NEAL SHUSTERMAN'S
DARKNESS CREEPING II

more tales to trouble your sleep

Illustrated by Barbara Kiwak

Lowell House
Juvenile
Los Angeles

CONTEMPORARY BOOKS
Chicago

OTHER BOOKS BY NEAL SHUSTERMAN

The Shadow Club

Kid Heroes

Dissidents

Speeding Bullet

What Daddy Did

The Eyes of Kid Midas

Darkness Creeping

Scorpion Shards

Publisher: Jack Artenstein
Vice President/General Manager, Juvenile Division: Elizabeth Amos
Director of Publishing Services: Rena Copperman
Editorial Director: Brenda Pope-Ostrow
Project Editor: Barbara Schoichet
Designer: Lisa-Theresa Lenthall
Production/Typesetting: Laurie Young

Lowell House books can be purchased at special
discounts when ordered in bulk for premiums and
special sales. Contact Department JH at the following address:

Lowell House Juvenile
2029 Century Park East
Suite 3290
Los Angeles, CA 90067

Manufactured in the United States of America

ISBN: 1-56565-285-1

Library of Congress Catalog Card Number: 95-21701

10 9 8 7 6 5 4 3 2 1

CONTENTS

RIDING THE RAPTOR   5

TRASH DAY   17

AN EAR FOR MUSIC   33

SOUL SURVIVOR   53

SECURITY BLANKET   67

GROWING PAINS   81

CONNECTING FLIGHT   95

CRYSTALLOID   109

To Kathy W. and Diane A.,
who inspire authors as well as students
—N.S.

RIDING THE RAPTOR

"THIS IS GONNA BE GREAT, BRENT!" SAYS MY OLDER brother, Trevor. "I can feel it."

I smile. Trevor always says that.

The trip to the top of a roller coaster always seems endless, and from up here the amusement park seems much smaller than it does from the ground. As the small train clanks its way up the steel slope of a man-made mountain, I double-check the safety bar across my lap to make sure it's tight. Then, with a mixture of terror and excitement, Trevor and I discuss how deadly that first drop is going to be. We're roller coaster fanatics, my brother and I—and this brand-new sleek, silver beast of a ride promises to deliver ninety incredible seconds of unharnessed thrills. It's called the Kamikaze, and it's supposed to be the fastest, wildest roller coaster ever built. We'll see . . .

We crest the top, and everyone screams as they peer down at the dizzying drop. Then we begin to hurl downward.

Trevor puts up his hands as we pick up speed, spreading his fingers and letting the rushing wind slap against his palms. But I can never do that. Instead I grip the lap bar with sweaty palms. And I scream.

You can't help but scream at the top of your lungs on a roller coaster, and it's easy to forget everything else in the world as your body flies through the air. That feeling is special for me, but I know it's even more special for Trevor.

We reach the bottom of the first drop, and I feel myself pushed deep down into the seat as the track bottoms out and climbs once more for a loop. In an instant there is no up or down, no left or right. I feel my entire spirit become a ball of energy twisting through space at impossible speeds.

I turn my head to see Trevor. The corners of his howling mouth are turned up in a grin, and it's good to see him smile. All his bad grades, all his anger, all his fights with Mom and Dad—they're all gone when he rides the coasters. I can see it in his face. All that matters is the feel of the wind against his hands as he thrusts his fingertips into the air.

We roll one way, then the other—a double forward loop and a triple reverse corkscrew. The veins in my eyes bulge, my joints grind against each other, my guts climb into my throat. It's great!

One more sharp turn, and suddenly we explode back into the real world as the train returns to the station. Our car stops with a jolt, the safety bar pops up, and an anxious crowd pushes forward to take our seats.

"That was unreal!" I exclaim, my legs like rubber as we climb down the exit stairs.

But Trevor is unimpressed.

"Yeah, it was okay, I guess," he says with a shrug. "But it wasn't as great as they said it would be."

I shake my head. After years of riding the rails, Trevor's become a roller coaster snob. It's been years since any coaster has delivered the particular thrill that Trevor wants.

"Well, what did you expect?" I ask him, annoyed that his lousy attitude is ruining my good time. "It's a roller coaster, not a rocket, you know?"

"Yeah, I guess," says Trevor, his disappointment growing with each step we take away from the Kamikaze. I look up and see it towering above us—all that intimidating silver metal. Somehow, now that we've been on it, it doesn't seem quite so intimidating.

Then I get to thinking how we waited six months for them to build it, and how we waited in line for two hours to ride it, and I get even madder at Trevor for not enjoying it more.

We stop at a game on the midway, and Trevor angrily hurls baseballs at milk bottles. He's been known to throw rocks at windows with the same stone-faced anger. Sometimes I imagine my brother's soul to be like a shoelace that's all tied in an angry knot. It's a knot that only gets loose when he's riding rails at a hundred miles an hour. But as soon as the ride is over, that knot pulls itself tight again. Maybe even tighter than it was before.

Yeah, I know what roller coasters mean to Trevor. And I also know what it means when the ride is over.

Trevor furiously hurls another baseball, missing the stacked gray bottles by a mile. The guy behind the counter is a dweeb with an Adam's apple the size of a golf ball that bobs up and down when he talks. Trevor flicks him another crumpled dollar and takes aim again.

"Why don't we ride the Skull-Smasher or the Spine-

Shredder," I offer. "Those aren't bad rides—and the lines aren't as along as the Kamikaze's was."

Trevor just hurls the baseball even harder, missing again. "Those are baby rides," he says with a sneer.

"Listen, next summer we'll find a better roller coaster," I say, trying to cheer him up. "They're always building new ones."

"That's a whole year away," Trevor complains, hurling the ball again, this time nailing all three bottles at once.

The dweeb running the booth hands Trevor a purple dinosaur. "Nice shot," he grunts.

Trevor looks at the purple thing with practiced disgust.

Great, I think. *Trevor's already bored out of his mind and it's only this amusement park's opening day.* As I watch my brother, I know what'll happen now; five more minutes, and he'll start finding things to do that will get us into trouble, deep trouble. It's how Trevor is.

That's when I catch sight of the tickets thumbtacked to the booth's wall, right alongside the row of purple dinosaurs—two tickets with red printing on gold paper.

"What are those?" I ask the dweeb running the booth.

"Beats me," he says, totally clueless. "You want 'em instead of the dinosaur?"

We make the trade, and I read the tickets as we walk away: GOOD FOR ONE RIDE ON THE RAPTOR.

"What's the Raptor?" I ask Trevor.

"Who knows," he says. "Probably some dumb kiddie-go-round thing, like everything else in this stupid place."

I look on the amusement park map but can't find the ride anywhere. Then, through the opening-day crowds, I look up and see a hand-painted sign that reads THE

RAPTOR in big red letters. The sign is pointing down toward a path that no one else seems to be taking. That alone is enough to catch Trevor's interest, as well as mine.

He glances around furtively, as if he's about to do something he shouldn't, then says, "Let's check it out."

He leads the way down the path, and as always, I follow.

The dark asphalt we are on leads down into thick bushes, and the sounds of the amusement park crowd get farther and farther away, until we can't hear them at all.

"I think we made a wrong turn," I tell Trevor, studying the map, trying to get my bearings. Then suddenly a deep voice booms in the bushes beside us.

"You're looking for the Raptor, are you?"

We turn to see a clean-shaven man dressed in the gray-and-blue uniform that all the ride operators wear, only his doesn't seem to be made of the same awful polyester. Instead his uniform shimmers like satin. So do his eyes, blue-gray eyes that you can't look into, no matter how hard you try.

I look at Trevor, and tough as he is, he can't look the man in the face.

"The name's DelRio," the man says. "I run the Raptor."

"What is the Raptor?" asks Trevor.

DelRio grins. "You mean you don't know?" He reaches out his long fingers and pulls aside the limbs of a dense thornbush. "There you are, gentlemen—the Raptor!"

What we see doesn't register at first. When something is so big—so indescribably huge—sometimes your brain can't quite wrap around it. All you can do is blink and stare, trying to force your mind to accept what it sees.

There's a valley before us, and down in the valley is a

9

wooden roller coaster painted black as night. But the amazing thing is that the valley itself is part of the roller coaster. Its peaks rise on either side of us in a tangle of tracks that stretch off in all directions as if there is nothing else but the Raptor from here to the ends of the earth.

"No way," Trevor gasps, more impressed than I've ever seen him. "This must be the biggest roller coaster in the world!"

"The biggest *anywhere*," corrects DelRio.

In front of us is the ride's platform with sleek red cars, ready to go.

"Something's wrong," I say, although I can't quite figure out what it is. "Why isn't this ride on the map?"

"New attraction," says DelRio.

"So how come there's no crowd?" asks Trevor.

DelRio smiles and looks through us with those awful eyes. "The Raptor is by invitation only." He takes our tickets, flipping them over to read the back. "Trevor and Brent Collins," he says. "Pleased to have you aboard."

Trevor and I look at each other, then at the torn ticket stubs DelRio has just handed back to us. Sure enough, our names are printed right there on the back, big as life.

"Wait! How did—" But before I can ask, Trevor cuts me off, his eyes already racing along the wildly twisting tracks of the gigantic contraption.

"That first drop," he says, "that's three hundred feet."

"Oh, the first drop's grand!" DelRio exclaims. "But on this ride, it's the last drop that's special."

I can see Trevor licking his lips, losing himself in the sight of the amazing ride. It's good to see him excited like this . . . and *not* good, too.

Every time DelRio talks I get a churning feeling in my gut—the kind of feeling you get when you find half a worm in your apple. Still, I can't figure out what's wrong.

"Are we the only ones invited?" I ask tentatively.

DelRio smiles. "Here come the others now."

I turn to see a group of gawking kids coming through the bushes, and DelRio greets them happily. The look in their eyes is exactly like Trevor's. They don't just want to ride the coaster—they *need* to ride it.

"Since you're the first, you can ride in the front," DelRio tells us. "Aren't you the lucky ones!"

While Trevor psyches himself up for the ride, and while DelRio tears tickets, I slip away into the superstructure of the great wooden beast. I'm searching for something—although I'm not sure what it is. I follow the track with my eyes, but it's almost impossible to stick with it. It twists and spins and loops in ways that wooden roller coasters aren't supposed to be able to do—up and down, back and forth, until my head gets dizzy and little squirmy spots appear before my eyes. It's like a huge angry knot.

Before long I'm lost in the immense web of wood, but still I follow the path of the rails with my eyes until I come to that last drop that DelRio claimed was so special. I follow its long path up . . . and then down. . . .

In an instant I understand just what it is about this ride I couldn't put my finger on before. Now I *know* I have to stop Trevor from getting on it.

In a wild panic I race back through the dark wooden frame of the Raptor, dodging low-hanging beams that poke out at odd angles.

When I finally reach the platform, everyone is sitting

in their cars, ready to go. The only empty seat is in the front car. It's the seat beside Trevor. DelRio waits impatiently by a big lever extending from the ground.

"Hurry, Brent," DelRio says, scowling. "Everyone's waiting."

"Yes! Yes!" shout all the kids. "Hurry! Hurry! We want to RIDE!"

They start cheering for me to get in, to join my brother in the front car. But I'm frozen on the platform.

"Trevor!" I finally manage to say, gasping for breath. "Trevor, you have to get off that ride."

"What are you nuts?" he shouts.

"We can't ride this coaster!" I insist.

Trevor ignores me, fixing his gaze straight ahead. But that's not the direction in which he should be looking. He should be looking at the track behind the last car—because if he does, he'll see that there *is* no track behind the last car!

"The coaster doesn't come back!" I shout at him. "Don't you see? It doesn't come back!"

Trevor finally turns to me, his hands shaking in infinite terror and ultimate excitement . . . and then he says . . .

"I know."

I take a step back.

I can't answer that. I can't accept it. I need more time, but everyone is shouting at me to get on the ride, and DelRio is getting more and more impatient. That's when Trevor reaches out his hand toward me, his fingers bone white, trembling with anticipation.

"Ride with me, Brent," he pleads desperately. "It'll be great. I can feel it!"

I reach out my hand. My fingers are an inch from his.

"Please . . ." Trevor pleads.

He's my brother. He wants me to go. They *all* want me to go. What could be better than riding in the front car, twisting through all those spins and drops? I can see it now: Trevor and me—the way it's always been—his hands high in the air, wrestling the wind, and me gripping the safety bar.

Only thing is, the Raptor *has* no safety bar.

I pull my hand back away from his. *I won't follow you, Trevor!* my mind screams. *Not today. Not ever again.*

When Trevor sees me backing away, his face hardens— the way it hardens toward our parents or his teachers or anyone else who's on the outside of his closed world. "Wimp!" he shouts at me. *"Loooooser!"*

DelRio tightly grips the lever. "This isn't a ride for the weak," he says, his hawk eyes judging me, trying to make me feel small and useless. "Stand back and let the big kids ride."

He pulls back on the lever, and slowly the Raptor slides forward, catching on a heavy chain that begins to haul it up to the first big drop. Trevor has already turned away from me, locking his eyes on the track rising before him, preparing himself for the thrill of his life.

The coaster clacketty-clacks all the way to the top. Then the red train begins to fall, its metal wheels throwing sparks and screeching all the way down. All I can do is watch as Trevor puts up his hands and rides. The wooden beast of a roller coaster groans and roars like a dragon, and the tiny red train rockets deep inside the black wooden framework stretching to the horizon.

Up and down, back and forth, the Raptor races. Time is paralyzed as its trainload of riders rockets through thrill after terrifying thrill, until finally, after what seems like

an eternity, it reaches that last mountain.

DelRio turns to me. "The grand finale," he announces. "You could have been there—*you* could have had the ultimate thrill if you weren't a coward, Brent."

But I know better. This time, *I* am the brave one.

The red train climbs the final peak, defying gravity, moving up and up until it's nothing more than a tiny red sliver against a blue sky . . . and then it begins the trip down, accelerating faster than gravity can pull it. It's as if the ground itself were sucking it down from the clouds.

The Raptor's whole wooden framework rumbles like an earthquake. I hold on to a black beam, and I feel my teeth rattle in my head. I want to close my eyes, but I keep them open, watching every last second.

I can see Trevor alone in the front car. His hands are high, slapping defiantly against the wind, and he's screaming louder than all the others as the train plummets straight down . . . into that awful destiny that awaits it.

I can see that destiny from here now, looming larger than life—a bottomless blacker than black pit.

I watch as my brother and all the others are pulled from the sky, down into that emptiness . . . and then they are swallowed by it, their thrilled screams silenced without as much as an echo.

The ride is over.

I am horrified, but DelRio remains unmoved. He casually glances at his watch, then turns and shouts deep into the superstructure of the roller coaster. "Time!"

All at once hundreds of workers crawl from the woodwork like ants. Nameless, faceless people, each with some kind of tool like a hammer or wrench practically growing from their arms. They all set upon the Raptor, dismantling it with impossible speed.

"What is this?" I ask DelRio. "What's going on?"

"Surely you don't expect an attraction this special to stay in one place?" he scoffs. "We must travel! There are worlds of people waiting for the thrill of a lifetime!"

When I look again at the roller coaster, it's gone. Nothing remains but the workers carrying its heavy beams off through the thick underbrush.

DelRio smiles at me. "We'll see you again, Brent," he says. "Perhaps next time you'll ride."

As the last of the workers carry away the final rail of the Raptor on their horribly hunched backs, I stare DelRio down. I can look him in the eyes now, unblinking, unflinching.

"Tell your friends about the Raptor," he says, then he pauses and adds, "No . . . on second thought, don't tell them a thing. Wouldn't want to spoil their surprise."

Then he strolls off into the dense bushes after the workers, who are carrying the Raptor off to its next location. I just stand there. Nothing is left but the breeze through the valley and the distant sounds of the amusement park far behind me.

No, I won't tell anyone—ever. What could I possibly say? And if I encounter the Raptor again someday, I can only hope I will have the strength to stare DelRio down once more, dig my heels deep into the earth beneath my feet . . . and refuse to ride.

TRASH DAY

IT BEGAN LONG BEFORE THAT *THING* ARRIVED ON their lawn.

In fact, it began long before Lucinda Pudlinger was born. There was no way to know all the strange and mysterious forces that had created the Pudlinger family. Nevertheless, all those forces bubbled and brewed together and spat out the Pudlingers on the doormat of humanity.

As for Lucinda, it had never really occurred to her how serious her situation was until the day Garson McCall walked her home from school.

"You really don't have to," Lucinda had told him, more as a warning than anything else. Still, Garson had insisted. For reasons that Lucinda could not understand, he had a crush on her.

"No," said Garson, "I really want to walk you home."

Lucinda didn't mind the attention, but she did mind the fact that Garson was going to meet her family. There was no preparing him for *that*.

As they rounded the corner on that autumn afternoon,

the Pudlinger home came into view. It was halfway down a street of identical tract homes—but there was nothing about where the Pudlingers lived that matched the other homes.

True, they had a small front lawn like every other house on the block, but on the Pudlingers' lawn there were three rusting cars with no wheels—and a fourth piled on top of the other three. The four useless vehicles had been there, as far as Lucinda knew, since the beginning of time. While others might keep such old wrecks with an eye toward restoring them, the Pudlingers, it seemed, just collected them.

There was also a washing machine on that lawn. It didn't work, but Lucinda's mom had filled it with barbecue ashes and turned it into a planter. Of course, only weeds would grow in it, but then weeds were Mrs. Pudlinger's specialty. One only needed to look at the rest of the yard to see that.

As for the house itself, the roof shingles looked like a jigsaw puzzle minus a number of pieces, and the pea-green aluminum siding was peeling (which was something aluminum siding wasn't supposed to do).

The Pudlinger place didn't just draw your attention when you walked by it. No, it grabbed your eyeballs and dragged them kicking and screaming out of their sockets. In fact, if you looked up "eyesore" in the dictionary, Lucinda was convinced it would say "See Pudlinger."

"Look at that place!" said Garson as they walked down the street. "Is that a house or the city dump?"

"It's *my* house," said Lucinda, figuring the truth was less painful when delivered quickly.

"Oh," replied Garson, his face turning red from the foot he had just put in his mouth. "I didn't mean there was anything *wrong* with it—it just looks . . . lived-in. Yeah, that's right—lived-in . . . in a homey sort of way."

"Homely" is more like it, thought Lucinda.

Out front there was a fifth rusty auto relic that still worked, parked by the curb. A pair of legs attached to black boots stuck out from underneath. As Garson and Lucinda approached, a boy of about fifteen crawled out from under the car, stood in their path, and flexed his muscles in a threatening way. He wore a black T-shirt that said DIE, and he had dirty-blond hair with streaks of age-old grease in it. His right arm was substantially more muscular than his left, the way crabs often have one claw much bigger than the other.

"Who's this dweeb?" the filthy teenager said through a mouth full of teeth, none of which seemed to be growing in the same direction. He looked Garson up and down.

Lucinda sighed. "Garson, this is my brother, Ignatius."

"My friends call me 'Itchy,'" (which didn't mean much, since Ignatius had no friends). "You ain't a nerd, are you?" Itchy asked the boy standing uncomfortably next to Lucinda.

"No, not recently," Garson replied.

"Good. I hate nerds." And with that, Itchy reached out his muscular right arm and shook Garson's hand, practically shattering Garson's finger bones. It was intentional.

"Hey, wanna help me chase the neighborhood cats into traffic?" Itchy asked. "It's a blast!"

"No thanks," said Garson. "I'm allergic to cats."

Itchy shrugged. "Your loss," he said, then returned to tormenting the fat tabby that was hiding under the car.

"What's with him?" asked Garson as he and Lucinda made their way toward the house.

Lucinda rolled her eyes. "He's been bored ever since he got expelled."

What Lucinda neglected to say was how happy her brother was to be out of school. He'd planned on getting out ever since last summer when he'd gotten a job operating the Tilt-A-Whirl at the local carnival. It was that job which had given him his powerful right arm. Pull the lever, push the lever, press the button—if he worked at it hard enough, and practiced at home, Itchy was convinced operating the Tilt-A-Whirl could become a full-time career. With a future that bright, who needed school?

"Lucinda!" shouted Itchy, still under the car. "Mom and Dad are looking for you . . . and they're mad."

Lucinda shrugged. That was no news. They were always that way.

She turned to Garson. "You don't have to come in," she said more in warning than anything else.

But Garson forced a smile. He was going to see this through to the end, no matter how horrible that end might be. And it was.

The inside of the Pudlinger home was no more inviting than the outside. It had curling wallpaper, brown carpet that had clearly started out as a different color, and faded furniture that would cause any respectable interior decorator to jump off a cliff.

Mr. Pudlinger was in his usual position on the recliner, with a beer in his hand, releasing belches of unusual magnitude. He stared at a TV with the colors set so everyone's face was purple and their hair was green.

"Where have you been?" he growled at Lucinda.

"Field hockey practice," she answered flatly.

"You didn't take out the trash this morning," he said, grunting.

"Yes, I did."

"Then how come it's full again?"

Lucinda glanced over to see that the trash can was indeed full—full of the usual fast-food wrappers, beer cans, and unpaid bills.

"You take that trash out before dark, or no allowance!" her dad yelled from across the room. It must have slipped his mind that Lucinda didn't get an allowance. Not that they couldn't afford it—they weren't poor. It was just that her mom and dad liked to "put money away for a rainy day." Obviously they thought there was a drought.

Mr. Pudlinger shifted in his recliner and it let out a frightened squeak the way recliners do when holding someone of exceptional weight. It wasn't that Lucinda's dad was fat. It would have been perfectly all right if he was *just* fat. But the truth was, he was also . . . misshapen. He had a hefty beer gut, and somehow that beer gut had settled into strange, unexpected regions of his body, until he looked like some horrible reflection in a fun-house mirror.

"What does your father *do?*" Garson asked as they stepped over the living room debris toward the kitchen.

"What he's doing right now," she replied. "That's what he does."

"No, I mean for a living," Garson clarified.

"Like I said, *that's* what he does." Lucinda then went on to explain how her father was hurt on the job six years ago, and how he had been home ever since, receiving disability pay from the government. "He calls it 'living off of Uncle Sam,'" said Lucinda. Of course, Mr. Pudlinger failed to tell Uncle Sam that he had completely recovered two weeks after the accident.

In the kitchen they ran into Lucinda's mom, who Lucinda had also wanted to avoid. The woman had a cigarette permanently fixed to a scowl that was permanently planted on her mouth, which was permanently painted with more lipstick than Bozo the Clown.

Lucinda reluctantly introduced her to Garson.

"Garson?" she said through her frowning clown lips. "What kind of stupid name is that?" Cough, cough.

"I'm named after my father," Garson replied.

"Yeah, yeah, whatever," she said and spat her gum into the sink, where it caught on the lip of a dirty glass. "You wanna stay for dinner, Garson?" she asked, batting her eyes, showing off those caterpillarlike things she glued to her lashes.

"What are you having?" he asked.

"Leftovers," she said flatly.

Garson grimaced. "Left over from what?"

Mrs. Pudlinger was stumped by that one. No one had ever asked that before. "Just leftovers," she said. "You know, like from the refrigerator."

"No thanks," said Garson. Clearly his survival instinct had kicked in.

Lucinda was beginning to believe that Garson would soon leave, and she would be spared any further embarrassment. But then her father called him over to the recliner.

"Hey, kid, I wanna show you a magic trick," Mr. Pudlinger said with a sly smile. Then he extended his index finger in Garson's direction. "Pull my finger," he said.

Garson did, and Mr. Pudlinger let one rip.

Lucinda watched tearfully as, moments later, Garson sprinted down the street, racing away from her horrible family. It was the last straw, the last time she would allow her family to humiliate her like this. Their reign of terror had to end.

Just as she turned to walk back into the house, a car swerved in the street, its tires screeching as it tried to avoid a cat. The cat, having just missed being flattened, leaped into the arms of an elderly neighbor woman across the street. She turned a clouded eye at Itchy, who had just climbed out from under a parked car, laughing.

"You monster!" the old woman screamed, shaking her cane at him. "You horrible, evil boy!"

"Ah, shut yer trap, you old bat," Itchy snarled.

"You're trash!" the old woman shouted. "Every last one of you Pudlingers. The way you keep your house—the way you live your lives—*you're all trash!*"

That's when Mr. Pudlinger came out onto the porch. It was the first time Lucinda saw him outside in months. He turned to Itchy, put a hand on the boy's shoulder, and as if speaking words of profound wisdom, said, "Don't let anyone who's not family call you trash."

And then he went across the street and punched the old lady out.

When Lucinda's salvation finally came, it came thundering out of nowhere at five in the morning. That's when a mighty crash shook the house like an earthquake, waking everyone up.

Furious to have been shaken awake, Mr. Pudlinger shuffled out of the bedroom with Mrs. Pudlinger close behind, her face caked in some sort of green beauty mud that actually looked less offensive than her regular face.

"What's going on around here?" bellowed Mr. Pudlinger. "Can't a man get any sleep?"

Lucinda wandered out of her bedroom, and Itchy—a true coward when it came to anything other than cats and nerds—came out of his bedroom and hid right behind her.

Together the family shuffled to the front door and opened it to find yet another object on their front lawn—a Dumpster.

Dark green, with heavy ridges all around it, the huge metal trash container was one of those large ones they used in construction—eight feet high and twenty feet long. Yet it seemed like no Dumpster Lucinda had ever seen before.

"Cool," said Itchy, who must have already been calculating a hundred awful ways the thing could be used.

Mr. Pudlinger scratched his flaking scalp. "Who sent a Dumpster to us?" he asked.

"Maybe the Home Shopping Network," suggested Itchy.

"Naah," said Mom. "I didn't order a Dumpster."

But it clearly was meant for them, because the name "Pudlinger" was stenciled on the side.

It's like a puzzle, thought Lucinda. *What's wrong with this picture?*

But there were already so many things wrong with the Pudlinger lawn that the Dumpster just blended right in. Slowly Lucinda went up to it. It looked so . . . heavy. More than heavy, it looked dense. She looked down to see a tiny hint of metal sticking out from underneath. The edge of a car muffler poked out like the wicked witch's feet beneath Dorothy's house.

Mrs. Pudlinger gasped. "Look!" she said. "It crushed the Volkswagen Itchy was born in!"

Mr. Pudlinger began to fume. "I'll sue!" he shouted. And with that he stormed back into the house and began to flip through the Yellow Pages in search of a lawyer.

The Dumpster caught the sun and cast a dark shadow. As Lucinda left for school that day, she couldn't help but stare at the thing as she walked around it to get to the street.

It's just a Dumpster, she tried to tell herself. The way she figured it, some neighbor—some *angry* neighbor—took it upon himself to provide a container large enough to haul away all the junk her family had accumulated over the years. But if that were so, then why didn't they hear the truck that brought it here?

Before Lucinda knew what she was doing, she had put down her books and was walking toward the gigantic green container. Slowly she began to touch it, brushing her fingers across the metal, then laying her hand flat against its cold, smooth surface. As she touched it, all thoughts seemed to empty from her mind. It was as if the Dumpster was hypnotizing her. She giggled to herself for thinking such a silly thought and stepped away from it.

Then the Dumpster shifted just a bit, and the dead Volkswagen Bug beneath it creaked a flat complaint. *Anything that crushes one of our lawn cars can't be all bad,* thought Lucinda with a chuckle.

No, Lucinda decided, this thing was not evil—far from it. In fact, to Lucinda it seemed almost . . . friendly—certainly more friendly than anything else on their poor excuse for a lawn. And clearly it seemed to be waiting. Yes, happily waiting for something . . . but what?

Whistling to herself, Lucinda turned away. And as she strolled off to school, she thought about the great green metal box and the way it sat in anticipation, like a Christmas present waiting to be opened.

The neighbor's fat tabby cat was sitting proudly on the hood of one of the lawn cars when Lucinda returned home that afternoon. The Dumpster hadn't moved.

All day Lucinda hadn't been able to get it out of her mind. It was as if the thing had fallen into her brain instead of onto their weed-choked lawn. In fact, she had actually looked forward to coming home, just so she could take a good look at it again. There was something noble about the way it stood there—like a silent monolith.

But it isn't silent, is it? Lucinda thought. There were noises coming from within its dark green depths—little scratches and creaks, like rats crawling around. *Is there something alive in there?* she wondered. *Is there anything in there at all, or is it just my imagination?*

If it had been a Christmas present Lucinda would have been able to shake it, feel its weight, and try to guess what it held. But there was no way she could lift a Dumpster.

Unable to stand not knowing what was inside, she ran to the porch and got several chairs and stacked them one on top of the other. Then she climbed the rickety tower she had created and peered over the edge of the Dumpster.

As she had expected, it wasn't empty, and the shock of what Lucinda saw nearly made her lose her balance and tumble back to the ground. But she held on, refusing to blink as she stared down into the Dumpster . . .

. . . at her father, who sat in his recliner, watching TV.

"Dad?" she shouted. "Dad, what are you doing?"

"What does it look like I'm doing?" he asked, clicking the remote control with the speed of a semiautomatic weapon. "Get me the TV program guide, or you're grounded!"

In another corner of the Dumpster sat Lucinda's mother, with her entire vanity and makeup collection before her. She scowled at her own reflection, took a deep drag of her cigarette, and began to apply a fresh layer of makeup.

"Mom?"

"Leave me alone," she said. "I'm having a bad hair day." Cough, cough.

In the third corner of the Dumpster stood Itchy. There was a lever coming from the metal floor, and a button on the wall. Pull the lever, push the lever, press the button. Pull the lever, push the lever, press the button—Itchy was working away.

"Have you all gone crazy?" yelled Lucinda. "Don't you know where you are?"

But it was clear that they didn't. Her father thought he was in the living room, her mother thought she was in the bedroom, and Itchy, well, he thought he was king of the Tilt-A-Whirl. They all were in their own private little heaven, if you could call it that. This Dumpster—this terrible, wonderful Dumpster—wasn't designed to haul away *things*—it was designed to haul away *people*!

"Well, are you coming inside or what?" asked her father.

Lucinda could have argued with them. And maybe, if

she tried hard enough, she could have broken through their little trances and made them come out.

But if she tried hard enough, she could also keep herself from telling them anything at all.

That thought brought the tiniest grin to her face—a grin that widened as she leaped to the ground, into a tangle of weeds that cushioned her fall. Her smile continued to grow as she stepped into the house, and she broke into a full-fledged laughing fit as she raced into her room and began to bounce on her bed.

The Dumpster was taken away sometime during the night.

The following week, Garson McCall stopped by to apologize for being so rude on his first visit. The startled look on his face didn't surprise Lucinda. She had many startled visitors during those first few days. One need only look at the car-less, freshly planted lawn to know something had changed.

"Hi, Garson," said Lucinda in a dark, sad tone that didn't seem to match the brightness of the spotless house.

"Wow! What an overhaul!" exclaimed Garson as he stepped inside, his eyes bugging out at the new carpet and furniture.

Lucinda just shrugged.

A fifteen-year-old kid came bounding out of the kitchen to greet him, wearing a million-dollar smile that showed perfect teeth. "Hi, Garson, what's up?" the boy asked.

"Itchy?" Garson murmured in disbelief.

"Ignatius," the clean-cut boy corrected. "But my friends call me Nate."

In the living room a man who looked like an athletic version of Mr. Pudlinger was sipping lemonade and reading *Parents* magazine. In the kitchen a woman who resembled Mrs. Pudlinger, with several coats of makeup peeled away, was baking a pie.

"Garson, would you like to stay for dinner?" asked the pleasant-looking woman. "We're having T-bone steak and apple pie!"

"Sure," said Garson.

Lucinda could practically see him drool, but the flat expression on her own face never changed. In fact, she didn't know if she *could* change it anymore.

"I can't believe these are the same people I saw last week!" whispered Garson excitedly.

"They're not," said Lucinda. "They're replacements sent by the Customer Service Department."

Garson laughed, as if Lucinda had made a joke, and Lucinda didn't have the strength to convince him it was true.

"Listen, Garson," she finally said. "I'd like to talk, but I can't. I have to study."

"Study?" Garson raised an eyebrow. "On a Saturday?"

"I have to get an A in math," Lucinda replied.

"And science," added the new Mrs. Pudlinger cheerfully.

"Don't forget English and history," Mr. Pudlinger sang out. "My daughter's going to be a straight-A student, just like her brother!"

Lucinda sighed, feeling herself go weak at the knees. "*And* I have to be the star of the field hockey team. *And* I have to keep my room spotlessly clean. *And* I have to do all my chores *perfectly* . . . or else."

"Or else . . . what?" asked Garson.

Then Lucinda leaned in close, and with panic in her eyes, she desperately whispered in his ear, "Or else it comes back for me!"

Mrs. Pudlinger turned from her perfect pie. "Lucinda, dear," she said with a smile that seemed just a bit too wide, "isn't it your turn to take out the garbage?"

"Yes, Mother," Lucinda replied woodenly.

Then Lucinda Pudlinger, dragging her feet across the floor like a zombie, took out the trash . . . being *horribly* careful not to let a single scrap of paper fall to the ground. Ever.

AN EAR FOR MUSIC

FOR LEE TRAN, MUSIC WAS ALL THERE WAS, AND ALL there would ever be. Nothing mattered but his music—and he let that thought swell his head as he stepped onto the stage of the huge concert hall, to the sound of thunderous applause.

The old woman was there.

Although the lights shone on his face, he could see her in the private box seat—a place reserved for only the wealthiest patrons of the arts. He could see the pearls around her neck, and her gown, which must have once been elegant, as she herself must have once been. But now she was old. Her face was wrinkled, her teeth yellow, and her thin gray hair wound in a bun so tight, it seemed to lift her ears toward the tip of her skull.

Lee pretended not to notice her. He knew how very important she was, but he wouldn't give her the pleasure of knowing that he cared.

The applause died down as he reached the front of the orchestra. With his bow in one hand, and his violin firmly wedged beneath his chin, he waited for the conductor to signal the beginning of the concerto—a concerto Lee had written himself.

While other thirteen-year-olds played video games, Lee wrote music. It wasn't his first concerto, but it was the first one that was actually being played by an orchestra. It was also the first time Lee would be the featured soloist in front of so many people. It would have terrified him if he weren't so completely sure of himself.

The conductor brought down his baton, and the piece began with a thundering of brass and the pounding pulse of strings. In a moment the piece was mellowed by the smooth flow of woodwinds, and finally, above it all, rose a single violin, singing to the immense darkened hall.

It was Lee. While the fingers of his left hand flew back and forth across the strings and his right hand gently brushed the bow back and forth, he was creating sound so perfect even the conductor was in awe.

The piece was hard, filled with complex fingering and musical changes so grand, there were very few people in the world who could even play it. Lee was one of them. Although this was the first time he played with a major symphony, there had been rumors about him. Rumors that he was not only the greatest young composer of the century, but also the finest violinist known today. He was a fresh discovery in the world of music—and thinking about it made him play even better.

He became one with the violin, his passion flowing through him, flowing through the instrument . . . and as he played, the temperature in the concert hall began to rise.

First it rose a half degree, then a full degree, then two

degrees at a time, until people began to feel uncomfortable. *Why is it getting so warm?* they were thinking. *Is the air-conditioning broken? Are there too many people crammed into the hall?*

These thoughts flitted through the dark hall, but they didn't linger for long. For the music was so perfect, so brilliant that there was no room left in anyone's mind to think of anything else.

The piece grew to its fabulous finale, and Lee's fingers began to move so fast that they became a blur. The audience sighed in ecstasy and gasped in joy . . . and then they screamed in terror as the carpet beneath them burst into flames.

The fire exploded all around Lee, but he couldn't stop playing. Even as the emergency sprinklers began to gush icy water, and the entire audience raced toward the fire exits in panic, he continued to play. All the other musicians ran from the stage—all but Lee. He alone remained onstage until the piece was over, and when the last note was played, the only ones left in the burning concert hall were his parents, who were onstage with him trying to drag him out, and the old woman, the one who had been sitting alone in her box seat. Yes, throughout the fire, she sat there, applauding as the sound of fire engines grew nearer, and the smoke and flames rose higher.

The woman came to Lee's home the next day. She wore a molting fur coat that smelled of mothballs, and it also had a trace of smoke left over from the fire the night before. The moment Lee laid eyes on her, he recognized the woman. She even wore the same clothes she'd worn to the concert.

Although she looked terribly out of place in the small, dingy apartment, the woman stepped in as if she belonged. Tall and intimidating, this woman somehow had a sense of royalty about her that Lee could not explain.

"Do you know who I am?" she asked his mother, who stood next to Lee staring at the stately woman.

"Of course we do, Madame Magnus," she answered. "How wonderful of you to come to visit Lee in his home." She cleared her throat nervously. "How terrible last night was," she began hesitantly, then didn't quite know what to say.

"Nonsense," said Madame Magnus. "The fire was put out, the concert hall was saved, and no one was hurt."

"But the show was ruined," said Lee's mother.

Madame Magnus smiled. "Ah . . . but what we *did* hear—it was heaven!" She turned to Lee. "You play like an angel, young Master Tran," she said. "More than an angel—a god."

Lee liked the sound of that but decided not to let it show. He shrugged. "I just play," he said simply.

Madame Magnus looked Lee over as if examining a horse. She touched his chin and lifted it, forcing him to look at her. Lee didn't like the feel of her fingers. They were like old newspapers left out in the rain that had crinkled up and dried in the hot sun.

"Play something for me, Lee," she said, as if it were a demand. "I would very much like to hear you again."

Lee did not like being treated like a trained seal, performing on request. He was an artist, and artists had to be treated with some respect. Even thirteen-year-old artists.

Most people couldn't understand what it meant to be a

musician. Lee's grandfather had, but he was long dead now. It was his grandfather who had given Lee his first violin when Lee was only four. While other kids were drooling at cartoons, Lee Tran had begun creating music.

Now that his grandfather was gone, there was no one else in the family who cared for music the way Lee did. His father was a poor man who worked hard and saw little in such frivolous things. As for Lee's mother, she had a tin ear and didn't know rock from Rachmaninoff. But one thing she did know—Lee had an inborn talent. And, thanks to her, Lee got his music lessons, even if the family had to go without food to pay for them.

In time, Lee became inseparable from his violin. Playing it was as important to him as breathing.

"No," he told Madame Magnus. "I don't feel like playing now."

Instantly his mother pulled Lee aside and whispered angrily into his ear. She spoke in her native Vietnamese, so the old woman couldn't understand, but Lee suspected that Madame Magnus knew the language, and perhaps many others.

"Lee," his mother told him. "This woman, she is rich. She gives money to musicians, and the school she runs is the best."

"I don't care about her money," Lee said.

"But you care about your music. Study with her, and you'll become great."

"I already am great," answered Lee matter-of-factly. "And besides, what if she doesn't choose me for this special school of hers?"

"She'll choose you," his mother said with a certainty that Lee could not deny. Turning from him, she went to the shelf and took down his violin. "Play, my son," she pleaded. "Melt this woman with your music."

Lee opened the violin case. The instrument lay there in its velvet-lined case, a small silent creature, beautiful and powerful. But before he could play, Lee had to have the answer to a single question. He looked up at his mother and asked: "What caused the fire last night?"

His mother shrugged. "Electrical wiring?" she suggested. "Or someone smoking where they should not have been?"

Her guesses were logical, but Lee had his own idea about it, though he didn't dare say it out loud. The fact was he had never played as well as he had last night, and although sometimes when he played he felt the room around him change, he had never seen his music produce a fire. So far he had noticed the lights dim or grow brighter when he played. Once he felt the air chill, and another time he had felt it grow warm. It always depended on the piece he was playing. But what he had felt last night was like nothing he had ever felt before. Did this Madame Magnus understand that?

"Play for her, Lee," his mother begged.

Finally Lee fit the violin into the nape of his neck and began one of his original melodies. It was brooding and fore-boding. It was dark and filled with solemn tones, and as he had done the night before, Lee forced his soul into the music, letting the sounds resonate through every bone in his body.

When he was done, and his musical trance cleared, Lee saw his mother and the old woman gaping at him. Outside, the sudden pitter-patter of rain was hitting the windows and rattling down the drainpipe from a sky that had been clear only five minutes ago.

The old woman smiled. "Will you come study with me at my school?" she asked.

Lee hesitated. Seeing the power he had in the moment, he milked it and held that power like a long musical note. Then he asked, "How good am I . . . really?"

"You are a master, young man," whispered the old woman. "You are among the best."

This was a good enough answer for Lee. Perhaps he would become famous. Perhaps he would become rich. He liked the idea of both. And if one of the steps along the way to the greatness he was destined for was studying with this ruined old woman, then he would take that step.

"Sure," he said. "I'll come to your school."

Madame Magnus clapped her hands together in joy. "We shall leave immediately," she said. "I pay all my students' expenses, and help support each of their families. Your parents shall receive five hundred dollars a week while you attend my school."

Lee's mother grabbed her heart. "You are far too generous, Madame Magnus," she said, her breath taken away.

But the old woman only smiled through her ancient stained teeth. "Oh, but he's worth much, much more."

The Magnus Conservatory of Music was on an estate in Northern Vermont. It was a three-story mansion, completely hidden by the dense woods around it and far from the troubles of the big city. As he and his new teacher stepped out of Madame Magnus's limousine, Lee took a good look at the sprawling stately structure. It seemed odd to Lee that something so huge and so finely crafted could be so far from civilization.

"The upper floor is where I live," explained Madame Magnus. "The rest of it is filled with classrooms and lodgings for my students." She smiled at her new pupil. "I have chosen forty-nine students to work with. *You* are the fiftieth."

Another boy, perhaps a year or two older than Lee, with small, round glasses came down the front steps to meet them.

"This is Wilhelm," said Madame Magnus. "He is your roommate. He is a star cellist who came all the way from Germany to study with me."

Before heading into the conservatory, Lee turned to look through a patch of woods, where he saw another building hidden deep within the tall trees. "What's out there?" he asked, pointing to the small wooden structure.

"The guest house," replied Madame Magnus. She said nothing more about it, but at its mention, Lee could see Wilhelm, who was already quite pale, grow even paler.

The work at the conservatory was grueling—the hours long, the classes hard. Madame Magnus taught all the musical classes herself, and for the "lesser subjects," as Madame Magnus called everything else, she had hired the finest instructors.

"Do you feel honored to be in my school?" she asked Lee after his first week.

Lee smiled slyly. "That depends," he said. "Do you feel honored to have *me* here?"

The old woman smiled back. It was a fine thing for Lee to finally have a teacher who thought the way he did—who knew music the way he did. Now he knew that Madame

Magnus was the greatest music teacher that ever was. Only she could show him that path to greatness he so desired.

Yes, Madame Magnus knew her music. In fact, she could teach every instrument and knew exactly what to say to her young musicians and composers to inspire them all to greatness. But her course of instruction for Lee was strange indeed. She would not let Lee play any of the pieces he knew, nor let him play anything he wrote himself. Instead, she set him to work on dull exercises—scales and fingering practice—terribly mundane exercises that he had outgrown the first week he'd picked up a violin.

Next she had him play musical pieces that seemed specifically designed to be emotionless. Lee was confused. She spoke to him of passionate music, and of achieving flawless control of his instrument, yet she specifically kept him from playing pieces that would inspire him. Lee complied with her wishes, and if he had been flawless before, these awful exercises made him beyond perfect.

Still, she kept his great musical abilities a secret from everyone else in the school, keeping him apart from the other students as if he were some kind of secret. Curious, Lee wondered what other secrets she kept.

Like the secret guest house.

More than once Lee had seen her personal butler go out there, and Lee began to feel a sort of kinship for the lonely little house kept separate from the rest of the school. For in a way, the guest house was like him, wasn't it? Everything inside it was kept hidden and locked up by Madame Magnus, the same way his talents were kept locked and hidden by her firm rule.

Once a week Madame Magnus's students gave her a personal concert, but Lee was not even allowed to play in these.

"You are only to watch," the old woman had told him, "and to listen."

Fuming, Lee would sit out in the audience with Madame Magnus, thinking of all the things he could do with the music that was being played.

I could bring forth flames or frost, he mused. *I could fill the room with steam or snow. Perhaps I could even drain the very air from the room.*

Could he do that? Lee would never really know as long as Madame Magnus refused to let him play.

During these weekly concerts he would watch the strange old woman. There was something unsettling about the way she listened—the way her ears perked up at every note she heard. It was as though she absorbed the sounds, as though they flowed into her ears like water rushing into a whirlpool. Week after week he observed his teacher practically sucking in the music. It reminded Lee of something, but he couldn't put his finger on it.

"Have you noticed that when you stand behind Madame Magnus at a concert, the music suddenly doesn't sound right?" Lee asked Wilhelm one day. "It's as though somehow all the best notes have been sucked right out of it."

"Everyone's noticed it," Wilhelm answered in his heavy accent. "The woman, she gives me the shivers. Still, she is the best teacher there is. She has told me that my playing will make me famous someday, and I believe her."

Lee frowned. She had never said anything like that to him.

That night, just as Lee fell asleep, it occurred to him

just what Madame Magnus reminded him of. She was like a vampire . . . but one that lived on something other than blood. *Is that possible?* Lee wondered. *Can someone actually live on music?* But the thought was lost in a swift current of nightmarish dreams.

"Somebody lives there, you know," whispered Wilhelm the next day during breakfast. "No one ever sees him come out, but he's there. Everyone knows it."

Wilhelm was talking about the guest house, of course. Through the window of their room, the two boys could see its blackened windows.

"The lights never go on," said Wilhelm, "but one of Madame Magnus's servants brings a large platter of food out there three times a day." The thin, pale cellist leaned closer to Lee. "I think there's a monster in there."

Lee wondered about what Wilhelm had said, and that night he snuck out of the institute and crossed the distance through the woods to the mysterious little building. He just had to know if anyone or any*thing* lived there.

The guest house loomed in the woods, unpainted and covered with ivy. As Lee approached, its black windows seemed like dead eyes to him, and he began to wonder what nature of beast was kept there.

Making his way around the back of the sad-looking building, Lee pushed away the thorny bushes that surrounded it, bushes that seemed to be protecting the little house from trespassers. When he came across a broken window, his suspicions were confirmed—the windows weren't just dark, they were painted over so that no light could get in . . . *or* get out.

Lee took a step closer, and just as he put his face near the broken glass to peer inside, a hand reached out and grabbed him by the shirt! It was an ancient, pasty hand, and it held him in a desperate grip.

"Leave this place," rattled a raspy voice attached to a body Lee could not see. *"Leave and don't come back. Don't you know what she is?"*

Lee would have screamed if he hadn't lost his voice in fear. Standing frozen in the grip of the bony hand, he now could see the eye of an old man through the hole in the window.

"Nero played his violin," the wrinkled figure said in a voice that seemed to come from the grave. *"He played his violin, and Rome burst into flames. From Nero's flames she was born."* The voice grew in intensity. *"And all the masters who died before their time—they did not die!"* Then, as quickly as it had shot out at Lee, the hand pulled back into the jagged hole and disappeared into the darkness.

His heart pounding, Lee ran back to the conservatory, raced to his room, and hid beneath his covers, as if mere sheets and blankets could possibly shut out what he had seen. "Nero was an emperor of Rome," Wilhelm explained the next day in the library. He showed Lee a drawing in a history book. "He was powerful, arrogant, and legend has it that he played his violin while the entire city burned to the ground."

Lee looked at the article Wilhelm referred to in the encyclopedia. "But it doesn't say that Nero's playing actually *started* the fire."

Wilhelm shrugged. "Maybe it did, maybe it didn't. No one knows for sure."

Lee wondered how great a musician would have to be to be able to set an entire city on fire with his music. How evil such a person would have to be. And then he remembered what the old man behind the broken window had said: *From Nero's flames* she *was born.* Could he have meant Madame Magnus? Was *she* a creature born from those evil flames?

Lee closed the book and told Wilhelm what the old man had said about all the masters who had died before their time. "What do you think he meant by saying they didn't die?" he asked.

Wilhelm took off his glasses and rubbed his eyes. "I don't know," he said.

"Well, I'm going to find out," said Lee. "If Madame Magnus wants me in this school, then she can't keep secrets from me."

Wilhelm shook his head. "I wish I could be like you."

Lee looked at his friend. *But you can't be,* he thought. *Because you can never be the musician that I am.*

When Lee stormed up the stairs into Madame Magnus's private residence, she didn't seem shocked to see him, or even surprised. She only smiled that sly yellow-toothed smile of hers, then said, "To what do I owe this unexpected visit, young Master Tran?"

Lee got right to the point. "I want to know about the man in the guest house. Who is he, and why doesn't he ever come out?"

Madame Magnus looked at Lee from her high-backed velvet chair. "You've only been here two months," she said.

"What has that got to do with anything?" Lee demanded.

"Two months is a short time, but you are a fast learner. Perhaps you are ready."

"Ready for what?" Lee demanded.

But Madame Magnus only smiled. "Would you like to meet him? The man in the guest house?"

Lee wasn't expecting that. "Uh, sure," he said, hesitantly. "Yeah, sure, I'd like to meet him."

And with that, Madame Magnus and Lee Tran walked into the chill of the night and far into the woods, until they reached the old guest house. The old woman unlocked the many locks on the door, and soon it creaked open into a musty world of old furniture that was kept in perfect condition. A grandfather clock ticked away, ominously marking the time.

"Did you think it would be a dungeon?" asked Madame Magnus, laughing when she saw the surprise on Lee's face.

And yet, in its own way, the place did have the feel of a dungeon about it.

There was music coming from a back room, and Lee wondered why he hadn't heard the music outside as they approached. Slowly he looked around, and then he understood the reason why—the windows weren't just painted black, they were padded thickly, so that no sounds could escape.

Now listening to the music carefully, Lee noticed that it sounded familiar, and yet it also sounded totally new.

With Madame Magnus on his heels, he followed the sound into a back parlor, done in red velvet—the same red velvet, Lee noticed, that lined his violin case. There, hunched over a grand piano, sat the old man who had grabbed Lee through the broken window. He was pouring his heart into the music. Yet, as beautiful as the music was, it somehow seemed old and tired to Lee, not unlike the man himself.

As Lee listened to him play, once again the familiarity of the music tickled the corner of his brain. The music was romantic and sentimental, perfectly composed. It sounded like Gershwin, Lee finally decided. But this was nothing Gershwin had written in the short thirty-nine years of his life.

Lee studied the ancient figure still playing away at the piano. The old man could have been a hundred by the looks of him. He glanced up from the keys, and upon catching a glimpse of Lee, he sighed, then returned to his playing.

"I've brought you a young friend," said Madame Magnus to the old man.

"Is he the one?" the old man replied.

"The finest violinist alive, and the finest young composer in the world," answered Madame Magnus. And as his teacher said this, Lee held himself up proudly.

The old man just looked away, then returned to his music.

"You'll have to excuse George," said Madame Magnus. "He's not used to visitors."

And then Madame Magnus did something strange. She went to the piano and closed the lid over the keys, so the old man could no longer play. "Time to rest, George," she said. "Time to rest."

The old man threw a sad look over at Lee and stood, his bones creaking. Then he went to lie down on the velvet sofa in the corner. He folded his hands over his chest, closed his eyes, and let out a singular long raspy breath. It didn't take long for Lee to realize that the old man had died.

Feeling panic beginning to set in, Lee turned in terrified awe to Madame Magnus. But she said nothing. She simply walked over to the fireplace and took down a dusty violin case from the mantel.

"For you," she said, opening the case to reveal a Stradivarius violin that must have been hundreds of years old. "It belonged to Mozart himself," Madame Magnus announced. "Take it."

She held the violin out to Lee, and although he felt afraid to even touch it, he could not refuse the magnificent instrument. To play a Stradivarius violin was the dream of a lifetime. *Could this truly have been Mozart's?* he wondered as he took the beautiful wooden instrument into his hands.

Madame Magnus produced a handwritten manuscript of music, aged and as yellow as her skin. "Play for me, Lee," she said. "Play like you've never played before."

And Lee did.

For the first time in months he launched himself into a real piece of music. The Stradivarius was magnificent, and the piece of music glorious. It sounded like Mozart, but like no Mozart Lee had ever heard before. It was a rich musical tapestry full of life and youth and joy. Lee lost himself in it. He felt his soul plunging into the music. And as he played something happened—not to the room, not to the air, but to Madame Magnus herself. With every note it seemed the life of the music poured into her; the youthful, joyous tones seemed to suck into her flesh as if she were some musical black hole.

Lee couldn't keep his eyes off the woman, and although terror began to fill him, he couldn't stop playing. No longer looking at the sheet of music, he played, his fingers flying over the strings, creating music fast and fiery—music that exploded out of the violin.

But nothing caught fire.

Now all the power of the music funneled right into Madame Magnus. Her eyes burned with its intensity. And to his horror, Lee saw that with each note, Madame Magnus grew younger—younger and more powerful.

Finally the piece ended, and Lee was drenched in sweat. Gasping for breath, he let the bow and violin fall to the floor, for they were burning his fingers.

Before him stood Madame Magnus, a young woman, now no older than twenty-five, and she threw back her head and laughed a hearty, horrible laugh.

Lee willed himself to run, but he just stood there, unable to move. Then, looking down at his legs, he saw that heavy metal shackles now fastened him in place.

"How marvelous!" Madame Magnus cried with delight. "How perfectly marvelous!"

"What's going on?" Lee demanded. "I don't understand!"

The young Madame Magnus smiled her sly smile, only now, on a much younger face, it seemed more than just sly—it seemed evil.

"Come, now," she said. "Don't play dumb with me, young Master Tran. You know precisely what's going on."

And Lee did, but he couldn't admit it to himself. He didn't dare.

"The other young musicians in this conservatory—none of them are good enough to feed me the truly powerful music I thrive on. I needed a great master—a *young* master, someone whose genius would fill my ears with the fresh fire of youth and make me young again. You are the one, Master Tran. *You* are the one I need."

Lee could only stand there, shaking his head. Not a single word rose to his lips.

"Oh, there have been others—*many* others," said Madame Magnus. "Mozart did not die young. He lived to be an old man . . . in my care, of course. And there was Schubert—he, too, grew old . . . with me. And of course you met dear Mr. Gershwin. As you saw, he didn't die young as the rest of the world thought . . . and neither will you."

"No!" screamed Lee. "I won't stay here!"

Then Madame Magnus stepped forward and looked deep into the boy's terror-stricken eyes. "You'll do *exactly* as I say," she said. "You'll do exactly as I say for the rest of your life, young Master Tran. You'll play and you'll write music for no one but me. You'll feed me with your music as the masters before you did. And your music will keep me young and strong . . . until it is used up."

Madame Magnus picked up the violin and bow, then put them back into Lee's hands. "Now play for me," she said, any kindness that had once been there now gone from her voice. "Play me something *you* wrote. Something with *power*."

With no other choice, Lee tucked the Stradivarius beneath his chin and began to play, and instantly he felt his music swallowed whole by Madame Magnus's hungry, hungry ears.

I am the greatest, Lee told himself, fighting back tears of terror. *I am the greatest in the world!*

But that didn't matter anymore, since no one else would ever hear him play. Now his music would have to be enough, because now music was all there truly was for Lee Tran . . . and all there would ever be.

SOUL SURVIVOR

WHAT I TELL YOU NOW YOU CAN NEVER TELL ANOTHER living soul.

It began as a dream—or what I thought was a dream. I was floating—rising higher and higher. Then, when I looked back, I could see someone lying in bed. It was a boy. Not just any boy—it was my own self, and I was lying in the stillness of sleep.

This was one of those dreams where you know you're dreaming—where you have your whole mind, not just part of it, to think things through and make sense of everything. An out-of-body experience—that's what they call it. And as it turns out, I picked just the wrong time to have one.

The room I was floating in was bright and clear, because dawn had already broken, and light was pouring in through the blinds. Then I heard a noise growing louder. I should have realized something was wrong by the way it sounded. It grated against the silence of the morning, but I was so wrapped up in floating around the room, I didn't notice until it was too late.

There was a mighty roar and a shattering of wood and metal. Then something hot and silver passed through me, and in an instant it was gone.

So was my body.

So was the entire second story of our house.

A moment later, the blast of a great explosion shook the air.

When we had first moved to this house, my parents had asked me if I wanted the bedroom upstairs or downstairs. I had chosen upstairs. Big mistake. With the second floor of the house torn away, I could see my parents below in their roofless bedroom, screaming. They weren't hurt. No, they were terrified—still not knowing what had happened, and not understanding why there was morning sky above them instead of their ceiling fan.

But I knew exactly what had happened. A jumbo jet had taken off half of our house just before slamming into the ground two streets away.

As for my body, well, I'm sure it felt no pain because it was over so quickly. Anyway, I wouldn't know because I wasn't there to feel it. Perhaps if it hadn't happened so quickly, I might have been drawn back into my body to die with it, but that's not what happened.

Now I'm alive, but with no body to live in.

Perhaps that's how ghosts are made.

I remember drifting into school the next day, going up to my friends and screaming into their faces that I was still here. But they couldn't see me or hear me. I also remember hovering among the flowers at my funeral, thinking that being there was the proper and respectable thing to do.

For many weeks after that, I drifted through the rooms of my uncle's house, where my parents were staying now that our house was destroyed. I stayed there, sitting on the couch and watching TV with them. I sat on an empty chair at the dinner table, day after day, yet they never knew I was there . . . and never would.

Soon my parents' grief was too much for me to bear. There was nothing I could ever do to comfort them. So I left.

You can't imagine what it's like to have lost everything. Losing your house, and your things, and your friends, and your family is all bad enough—but to lose yourself along with it—*that* was beyond imagination. To lose my thick head of hair that I never liked to brush. To lose those fingernails that I still had the urge to bite. To lose the feeling of waking up to the warm sun on your face. To lose the taste of a cold drink, and the feel of a hot shower. To just *be*, with no flesh to contain your mind and soul. It was not a fun way to be.

I drifted to the lonely basement of an old abandoned building, and lay there for weeks, not wanting to go anywhere, not wanting to face a world I could not be part of. I just wanted to stay in that lonely place forever.

Perhaps that's how buildings become haunted.

It was months before I could bring myself to look upon the light of day again, and when I did, it was like coming out of a cocoon. Once I could accept that my old life was gone, I began to realize that I did have some sort of future, and I was ready to explore it.

I began by testing my speed. I was just an invisible

weightless spirit of the air, but I could will myself to move very fast. I practiced, building my skill of flight the way I had built my swimming speed in the pool—back in the days when I was flesh and bone. It wasn't that different, really, except now I didn't need muscles to make myself move, only thoughts.

Soon I could outrace the fastest birds and fly higher than the highest jets. I could turn on a dime and crash through solid rock as if I were diving through water. These were times I did not miss the heavy weight of my body.

And, wow—were there ever places to explore! I dove through the oceans, and actually moved through the belly of a great white shark. I dipped into the mouth of a volcano, racing through its dark stone cap—right into red-hot magma! I plunged deeper still, beyond the Earth's mantle to hit its super-dense core. It wasn't as easy to move through as water and air, but I did it. I did all of these things!

And each time I would slip into one of these great and magical realms, I would play a game with myself.

"I am this mountain," I would say. Then I would expand myself like a cloud of smoke, until I could feel my whole spirit filling up the entire mountain—from the trees at its base, to the snow on its peak.

"I am this ocean," I would say. Then I would spread across the surface of the water, stretching myself from continent to continent.

"I am this planet," I would tell myself, stretching out in all directions until I could feel myself hurtling through space, caught in orbit around the sun.

But soon the game lost its joy, for try as I might, I could never stay in the place where I had put myself. I did not want to be a mountain, immense and solitary, moving only when the earth shook. I did not want to be a sea, rolling uneasily toward eternity, a slave of the moon and its tides. I did not want to be the Earth, alone and spinning in an impossibly vast universe.

And so I dared to do something I hadn't found the nerve to do before. I began to move within the minds of human beings.

Like anything else, it took practice.

When I first slipped inside a human being, all I could see was the blood pumping through thousands of veins and arteries. All I could hear was the thump of a heartbeat. But soon I would settle within someone and begin to pick out a thought or two. And soon after that, I could hear all of that person's thoughts. Then I began to feel the things the way that person felt them, and see the world through that person's eyes—without ever letting on that I was there.

It was almost like being human, and this hint of being human again drove me on with a determination I'd never felt before.

After many weeks of secretly dipping into people's minds, I discovered I could not only hear the thoughts of these people but change those thoughts. I could make them turn left instead of right. I could make them have a sudden craving for an ice-cream sundae. Have you ever had a thought that seemed to come flying out of nowhere?

Perhaps someone was passing through you.

I moved daily from person to person, taking bits of knowledge with me as I went, taking memories of lives I'd never lived. I got to dive off cliffs in Mexico, experience the excitement and terror of being born, and I even blasted into space in a rocket, hiding deep within the mind of an astronaut.

This was a game I could have enjoyed forever . . . if I hadn't gotten so good at it. You see, I came way too close to the minds on which I hitchhiked.

"Who are you?"

The voice came as a complete surprise to me. I didn't know what to do.

"Who are you?" he demanded. "And why are you in my head?"

I was in the mind of a baseball player. I'd been there for a few weeks, and this was the first time he'd spoken to me.

He was a rookie named Sam "Slam" McKellen—I'm sure you've heard of him. They called him Slam because of the way he blasted balls right out of the stadium at least once a game. I know because I swung the bat with him.

"You'd better answer me," his thoughts demanded.

McKellen was the first one to know I was there. I was thrilled . . . but also terrified.

"My name is Peter," I said, and then I told him about the plane crash. I explained how I had lost my body, and how I had survived for more than a year on my own. I must have gone on babbling for hours—it was the first time I had someone to talk to.

McKellen listened to all I had to tell him, sitting quietly in a chair. Then, when I was done, he did something amazing. He asked me to stay.

"We have batboys in the dugout to help us out," he told me. "Who says I can't have a batboy on the *inside* as well? Heck, I'm important enough." He began to smile. "Sure," he said, "someone to pick up my stray thoughts that happen to wander off. Someone to remind me when I'm late, or when I forget something important. Sure, stay, kid," he said. "Stay as long as you want."

I don't need to tell you how it changed my life. It's not everyone who gets to live inside a major league baseball player. I mean, I was with Slam every time he swung that bat, every time he raced around those bases, every time he slid into home. And when he came up to accept his MVP trophy that year—it was *our* hands that held it in the air.

When we went out to eat, sometimes he would let me take over, giving me total control of his body. That way *I* could be the one feeding us that hot-fudge sundae—and tasting every last bit of it.

At night we would have long conversations about baseball and the nature of the universe—a silent exchange of thoughts from his mind to mine. In fact, we did this so often our thoughts were beginning to get shuffled, and I didn't know which were his thoughts and which were mine. Pretty soon I figured our two sets of thoughts and memories would blend together forever, like two colors of paint. As far as I was concerned, that would be just fine.

But then one day he offered to do something for me that I never had the nerve to ask him to do, and it changed everything.

"I'm gonna write your parents a letter," he announced. "I'm gonna tell them that you're alive and well and living inside my head."

I should have realized how that letter would have sounded, but I was too thrilled by the offer to think about what might happen. So we wrote the letter together and mailed it. Then, three days later, the world came collapsing down around us like a dam in a flood.

You see, my parents were never much for believing anything they couldn't see with their own eyes. When they got the letter, they called the police. The police called the newspapers, and suddenly the season's star MVP was a nut case who heard voices.

Sam "Slam" McKellen became the overnight laughing-stock of the American League. It's funny how that happens sometimes . . . but it wasn't funny to us.

I tried to get him to shut up, but he insisted on telling it like it is, getting up in front of the microphones and explaining to the world how a kid was renting space in his brain. We even went to see my parents, and although I kept feeding him facts about my past that only I could know, my parents were still convinced McKellen was a madman.

We were sent to doctors. Then we were put in hospitals and filled with so much medication, that sometimes it seemed like there was a whole platoon of us in here, not just two.

In the end Slam finally broke.

"Peter, I want you to leave," he told me as we sat alone in the dark, in the big house our baseball contract had bought. Our hair was uncombed and our face was unshaved for weeks.

"The doctors are right," Slam announced. "You don't exist, and I won't share my mind with someone who does not exist."

I could hardly believe what I was hearing.

"I order you to leave and never come back," he said. "Never look for me. Never talk to me. Never come near my thoughts again." And then he began to cry. "I hate you!" he screamed—not just in our head, but out loud. "I hate you for what you've done to me!"

I could have left then. I could have run away to find someone else who wouldn't mind sharing his life with a poor dispossessed soul like myself. But I realized that I didn't want to leave.

And I didn't want to share anymore, either.

"I'm not leaving," I told him. "*You* are."

That's how the battle began.

A tug of war between two minds in one brain is not a pretty sight. On the outside our face turned red, and our eyes went wild. Our legs and arms began convulsing as if we were having an epileptic fit.

On the inside we were screaming—battling each other with thoughts and fury. His inner words came swinging at me like baseball bats. But I withstood the blows, sending my own angry thoughts back like an iron fist, pounding down on him. Yes, I smashed that thankless baseball player with my ironfisted thoughts again and again, until I could feel myself gaining control. This was my body now. Not his. Not his ever again.

I pounded and pounded on his mind and filled his brain until there was no room for him anymore. But try as I might, I could not push him out. I could only push him *down*. So I pushed him down until the great baseball player was nothing more than a tremor in my right hand.

I had control of everything else . . . but even that

wasn't good enough. As long as any part of him was still there, he could come back, and I didn't want that. I had to figure out a way to get rid of him—for *good*.

That's when I remembered the dolphins.

In all my travels through air, land, and sea, there was only one place I knew I had to stay away from.

The mind of the dolphin.

I came close to the mind of a dolphin once. I had thought I might slip one on for size—but the place is *huge*! A dolphin's brain is larger than a human's, and its mind is like an endless maze of wordless thought.

When I had first neared a dolphin, I had felt myself being pulled into that mind, as if it were a black hole. I resisted, afraid I would get lost in there—*trapped* in there, wandering forever through a mind too strange to fathom.

And so I had turned away from the creature before I had been caught in its unknowable depths.

But now I had to find a dolphin again.

With the baseball player's spirit still making my hand quiver, I made a two-hundred-mile trek to Ocean World—a great marine park where they had countless dolphins in captivity. The whole time I didn't dare sleep, sure that the baseball player would fight his way back in control of my new body.

I arrived at midnight, on a day when a full moon was out and the empty parking lot was like a great black ocean.

With the strong body of the athlete I possessed, I climbed the fence and made my way to the dolphin tanks.

The plan was simple—I had worked it out a dozen times on my way there, and I knew that nothing could go wrong. I was stronger than the baseball player—I had already proven that. All that remained was getting him out of this body forever. Then, and only then, would it truly be mine.

I held on to that thought as I dove into the frigid water of the dolphin tank. Then, as I began to sink, I let Slam climb back into my mind. He was crazed now, screaming in anger and fear. He did not know what I was about to do, because I had kept my thoughts from him.

Suddenly there was a dolphin swimming up to us. It appeared to be just curious as to what was going on in its tank. As it drew near, and nearer still, I waited. Then when it was right up next to us, I blasted the baseball player out of my mind.

Though I'd tried many times to do that, this time it wasn't hard at all. In fact, it was as easy as blowing a feather out of my hand—because *this* time there was a place for his spirit to go. It went into the dolphin . . . and there it stayed.

But the dolphin clearly did not want that kind of company. It began to swim around the huge tank, bucking and twisting as if it could shed this new spirit that had merged with its own. But the dolphin's efforts were useless. Slam was now a permanent resident in the dolphin's mind.

And as for me—I was free! I was the sole owner of this fine body! All I had to do was swim back to the surface to begin my new life.

All I had to do was swim.

All I had to do . . .

That's when I discovered that this strong athletic body, this body that had hit a hundred fastballs over the right-field wall . . . had never learned to swim.

Slowly panic set in. I moved my hands, I kicked my legs, but the muscles in my body had no memory of how to behave in water. They thrashed uselessly back and forth, and my lungs filled with the icy water. Meanwhile the dolphin swam furiously around the tank, not caring about me or my new body, but trying to rid the foreign spirit that had entered its mind.

I felt death begin to pound in my ears with the heavy beat of my slowing heart, and I knew that if I didn't leave this body soon, it would be too late.

I had to leap out of it. I *had* to give it up. If I stayed in this body a few minutes longer, I might not have been able to escape it—I might have been bound to it the way normal people are bound to their bodies. But my will was strong, and my skill at body-jumping well honed.

And so I tore myself from my new body, letting my spirit float to the surface like a buoy . . . while there, at the bottom of the dolphin tank, the soulless body of the great baseball player drowned.

I don't know what happened after that, because I left and didn't look back. I have heard tales, though, of a dolphin who leaped out of its tank so often that they had to put a fence over it. But who knows if stories like that are ever true?

And that brings me to you.

You see, I've been with you longer than you think. I've been sitting on your shoulder watching what you do, what you say, and even how you say it. I know the names of your relatives. I know your friends. We've already shared several hot-fudge sundaes together.

And if someday very soon, you wake up only to find yourself walking toward a dolphin pool in the dead of night . . . don't worry.

Because I know you can swim.

SECURITY BLANKET

I FINALLY SNAPPED ON THE DAY WE FOUND THE QUILT.

It was 7:30 on a Saturday morning as we drove in the van searching for garage sales. As usual, Timmy and Maddie, my twin brother and sister, were fighting like Velociraptors in the back of the van, gouging each other's faces, ready to draw blood. I knew the fight would go on until one bit the other hard enough to make them let out a scream that could shatter bulletproof glass.

Dad had the music turned up full blast. It was his defense against Timmy and Maddie's little war. Today it was about their stupid yellow blanket. There used to be *two* stupid yellow blankets, but last year one got lost. Ever since, the surviving one was fought over constantly.

"Mom, can't you shut them up?" I asked.

Mom turned around and said something totally useless to the twins, like "You stop that now," then she went back to looking out the window for garage sale signs.

"Mom, I swear if they don't stop screaming, I'm going to gag them with that miserable blanket," I warned.

"Have some patience, Marybeth," Mom said, as she always says. "They're only five; they'll grow out of it." That's what she said when they were four, and when they were three, and when they were—

Two minutes later, Timmy bit Maddie, who then let loose a wail that rattled my brain. And that's when I did it: I grabbed their stupid yellow blanket, balled it up, and hurled it out my window. We were driving over a bridge, and the blanket went sailing like a comet over the edge of the guardrail, down to the creek below.

Now they both began to cry hysterically, and Mom looked at me horrified. "Marybeth, how could you do that? How could you be so cruel?"

I shrugged. "Maybe it's genetic," I said. Mom has yet to come up with a good comeback line to that one.

We continued on in a whimpering sort of silence until hand-painted signs led us into a neighborhood I didn't know. We found the garage sale at the end of the street.

A man and woman had all the leftovers of their life spread out on their driveway. They smiled when they saw us coming. People who give garage sales love when people drive up in nice big vans like ours. Vans can haul off a lot, and often we did.

It used to be that we mostly picked things up for the church thrift shop. But ever since Dad lost his job, we've been picking up things for ourselves. Usually people just get rid of junk at these sales, but every once in a while you can find something great. That's how we found my piano last month. It cost two hundred dollars, but the same one would have cost at least a thousand in a store.

But there were few such bargains at this garage sale.

"Most of the stuff we just pulled out of the attic," said the pale, thin woman who owned the house. "We hadn't been up there for years. It's funny the things you collect."

Yeah, I thought. *It's funny the things people try to get money for, too.*

Mostly it was clothes—old bell-bottom pants, stained blouses, moldy things that smelled of mothballs, and children's clothing. In fact, there were all kinds of children's things— toys, picture books . . . and a child's quilt.

The quilt was just draped there, over a little white rocking chair, and my eyes were immediately drawn to its lively colors. At first I thought it was because the sun was hitting it, shining through the trees, creating a patch of bright light that made the quilt seem to glow. But then I realized that the morning sun was still behind the clouds.

I stared, unable to take my eyes off the bright colors of the little blanket. *How could someone have sewn something so beautiful?* I wondered. And then I remembered how my grandmother used to sit hour after hour, working on patch-work quilts in tranquil silence. I'm not a sentimental type— things that are cute or quaint usually make me sick. But that quilt went beyond being quaint . . . it was masterful.

"Have your children grown and left home?" my mother asked the woman who lived there. "Is that why you're selling all of this?"

The woman just stared at her, blinking. "No, we don't have any children," she said.

"So what's the deal with all these toys?" I asked.

The woman shrugged uncomfortably. "I don't know. They were all up in the attic."

"They must have been left by the previous owners," my

mother suggested as she looked at the toys.

"Yes," said the woman. "Yes, that must be it." And then she left to help some other customers.

At the edge of the driveway, the twins bounced up and down on a plastic teeter-totter. But it wasn't long before they began teasing one another, and Dad had to pull them apart before they tore each other to shreds.

By now, the quilt had caught Mom's attention. "How beautiful," she said, lifting it off that little white chair. She unfolded it, revealing swimming colors and hundreds of bright patches of fabric. Then she turned to the woman and held it up. "How much for this?" she asked.

"Five dollars," the woman suggested.

"Sold," Mom said. Then she turned to me. "Pay for it, Marybeth. I believe you owe the twins a replacement blanket."

On Monday, during lunch, I sat with my friend Corinne in the cafeteria. We were scarfing down ravioli that was so salty, it made our eyes water.

"My little brother's a nuisance, too," Corinne said. "He gets into my things and makes paper airplanes out of my homework. Then, when I yell at him about it, he cries, and I end up getting in trouble. Is that what it's like with the twins?"

"It's different with them," I said. "It's not that they get into my things, it's just that they're, well, *there*."

"I wish my brother was just *there*," said Corinne. "Actually . . . I wish he *wasn't*." And then she laughed, smiling with a ravioli-filled mouth as if she were just making a joke.

But I knew she meant what she said, even if she didn't know it . . . because lots of times I felt that way, too.

When I got home that day, as I was walking down the hallway toward my room, I thought I saw something move. It was something about the size of a cat—or maybe it was just my imagination. Still, I had to investigate.

Mom was off at work, Dad was at a job interview, and the twins were at day care, so I was totally alone. Maybe I should have been scared as I stepped into the twins' room, looking for that moving shape, but I wasn't. Not yet, anyway.

As my eyes scanned the room, I saw that the blinds were drawn, casting diagonal slits of light against the wall. I also noticed that the quilt, which had been folded at the end of Timmy's bed when I left for school, wasn't there anymore. And then I saw it.

There, in the corner of the room, something was peering out at me. It was a creature with a dark face and many legs, like a scorpion—at least that was what I thought before my brain kicked in. Then I realized it was just a trick of the light. I quickly fumbled with the blinds, and they rose with a clatter, letting in the late afternoon sun. That's when I saw that there was no creature on the floor. It was just the quilt, crumpled into a random pile of hills and valleys, that when lit just right, seemed to be a living thing.

Still, I hesitated before I reached for it. Then I realized how silly I was being, so I grabbed it and shook it out to convince myself there was nothing hiding beneath it. Of course, nothing did shake out but a fine spray of dust that drifted in and out of the shafts of sunlight. I spread the quilt across Timmy's bed, then stood back to admire the way the light was hitting it.

There was something about the quilt that I hadn't noticed before. It wasn't simply a random patchwork of designs—each square was a scene. I had to look at it for a long time to really see it, but once I did, I couldn't deny that there were almost a hundred different scenes on that blanket. There was a winter scene of children playing in the snow, and a summer scene of children playing on the beach. Another square, which at first glance seemed to be just brown strips across a blue background, was actually someone crouching in the branches of a tree against a clear sky.

There were faces in the quilt, too, and after a while I began to feel the faces were all looking back at me. Suddenly it seemed there were a hundred people in the twins' room— all of them staring at me—and I could swear those faces were opening their mouths, trying to tell me something. But there was only silence.

I backed away from the quilt until I hit a picture on the wall, and it fell down. I picked up the picture, and when I looked back at the quilt, it was just a quilt again. No faces, just colorful fabric filling the many squares.

I left the twins' room with a shudder and went into the living room, where the only faces looking at me were those in the smiling family photos on the wall. Then I sat at my piano and played something soothing. It had all been my imagination, I told myself. And I kept telling myself that until I almost believed it.

It was only a matter of time until Maddie and Timmy had a fight over the quilt. They had shared it for two whole days before they got tired of sharing. It was actually a record for them.

It began at dawn.

"It's mine!" yelled Maddie.

"No, it's mine!" screeched Timmy.

"No, it's *mine!*"

"No, it's *MINE!*"

"NO, IT'S **MINE!**"

It would have gone on like that for hours if someone didn't stop them, so I scraped myself out of bed and went into their room.

"Will you two just SHUT UP!" I roared as Mom came into the room as well.

"Marybeth," she said, "we don't use the 'S' word in this house."

I smirked at her. "That's not the 'S' word," I said.

"Yeah," said Timmy. "*Stupid* is the 'S' word."

"It's MINE," said Maddie, returning to the war at hand. "It's for *me* to sleep with at night." She wrapped herself in the quilt, but Timmy grabbed a corner and tugged until Maddie spun out of it like a top and hit the wall with a *thud*.

"I've got an idea," I said, leaving the room and returning with thumbtacks. I pulled the quilt away from Timmy and tacked its four corners to the wall.

"Wonderful," said my mother, smiling at me with approval. "It was too pretty to sit on a bed anyway."

The twins began to whine about it, and that's when I left for my own room, where I dressed and left for school as quickly as I could. All the while, I was trying to push what I was thinking out of my mind. It was something I heard—not with my ears, but in a place deep within my head that my ears couldn't reach.

It was coming from the quilt. The moment that I had

driven those four thumbtacks through its corners, I had heard the quilt scream.

The next night Mom and Dad had a fight. Dad was doing his taxes and had papers spread across every table in the house. He always got irritable around tax time, but this year was worse than any other, because he had been out of work for so long.

He and Mom argued that night about money. They argued about how hard Dad was looking for work, and they argued that Mom didn't get paid enough. They also argued over the fact that they were arguing. Finally I heard my name mentioned, and I stood at the edge of my doorway looking out into the living room, listening to what they were saying.

"We can't have both," said my dad. "It's got to be one or the other."

"Well, we can't just take it away from her," said my mom. "She's wanted one for so long."

"Well, then, what are we going to do?" asked my dad in frustration. "Let the twins run around in the street after kindergarten?"

I knew what they were talking about. My piano. Ever since I was ten, they'd promised me I could have one, and just one month ago I finally got it. Now they were talking about selling it to pay for the twins' day care.

I didn't want to stand there and listen to their decision. I knew what it would be. The twins always got what they wanted. They were always taken care of first. And as for me, well, I would just have to share in Mom and Dad's money misery, because misery loves company, right?

Then Mom and Dad began to whisper so quietly that I couldn't hear, and I heard them coming into my room. I jumped onto my bed and pretended to read.

Mom, I could tell, almost had tears in her eyes. Dad looked pale and tired. *This is all the twins' fault,* I thought. Dad had lost his last job because he had to spend so much time at home when they had the chicken pox.

"Your father and I are going out," Mom said. "You'll watch the twins for us, okay?" She didn't so much ask me as tell me.

You must be desperate if you're asking me, is what I wanted to say. They never trusted me alone with the twins, because they said I was too mean to them, and they're probably right.

"Sure," I said. "I'll watch them."

As soon as the twins heard that they were being left with me, they began to whine.

"No!" Timmy yelled. "Marybeth will play tricks on us!"

"She'll play scary games," Maddie cried. "She'll make us cry. Marybeth hates us."

"Don't be silly," Mom said. "Marybeth's your sister. She loves you." And with that she and Dad left.

Now, I wouldn't say I'm the nicest person in the world, but I would never call myself evil. At least not until that night. I'm not sure what came over me, but as soon as Mom and Dad left, I turned to the twins with a big smile that was not meant to comfort them.

"All right, you two," I said. "Would you like to play a game?"

They looked at me with wide eyes that were getting wider by the second. "What kind of game?" they asked in unison.

"The monster game," I replied.

"No!" they cried. "We hate the monster game! We hate it!"

"Well, tough," I told them. "That's the game I want to play."

Immediately the twins ran into the living room and ducked under the coffee table, as if hiding there would keep them safe.

"Please, Marybeth," Timmy whimpered. "Please don't scare us!"

I dug through my closet until I found this wonderfully hideous rubber Halloween mask. Then I put it over my face and stomped out into the living room.

"*Grrrrrrowl!*" I roared, shoving my monster face under the coffee table. The twins ran screaming into our parents' room, and I stomped after them.

"I'm the monster that eats bad little boys and girls!" I growled, finding them in Mom and Dad's bed, hiding their faces with pillows.

"*Grrrrrrowl!*" I roared again. They screamed, leaped out of the bed, and ran. I stomped after them and found them in their own room. They were fighting to get underneath the quilt, which now lay crumpled in the corner of Timmy's bed, like a creature ready to spring.

That's odd, I thought. *Mom must have pulled it down from the wall.*

They grabbed the quilt and managed to wrap both of themselves in it from head to toe. I began to laugh at the way they quivered beneath it. I mean, did they think that a puny little blanket could protect them?

"Are you scared?" I growled at them.

"Yes, yes, we're scared."

"Are you *really* scared?"

"Yes!" they yelled. "Please stop, Marybeth!"

"Good!" I bellowed. "That's what you get for ruining everything for everyone."

Then they started to cry, and I realized I had gone too far. I took the dumb old mask off. "Oh, stop whimpering," I said. "It was just a game. You can come out now."

But they didn't come out.

"Come on," I coaxed. "You can't hide under that blanket all night!"

"We're not hiding," said Timmy. "We can't get out!"

I watched as the two of them struggled to unravel themselves from the blanket.

"Don't be ridiculous," I said. But as I watched them struggle, I could see the blanket stretching around them, pulling tighter and tighter—actually straining to keep them from struggling out.

"Help us, Marybeth!" they cried. "The monster—it has us! It's eating us!"

That's when I saw the eyes. They were attached to all those faces—hundreds of them—all staring out of the quilt . . . and this time I knew it wasn't just my imagination.

They were all the faces of children.

"Help us, Marybeth!" the twins kept shrieking.

Panicked, I ran across the room and, in the process, stepped on the thumbtacks which had held the thing to the wall. Wailing in pain, I fell to the ground. That's when I noticed that the twins' cries seemed to be getting weaker. I *had* to get to them out.

I crawled to the bed where the quilt still had them

wrapped up tighter than ever. I could see that, all bundled up, the thing did look like a creature . . . but like no creature I had ever imagined. I bit back my own fear, reached for the terrible quilt, grabbed ahold of an edge, and tore it off the bed.

But there was nothing beneath it.

There in my hand was a mere blanket, a limp quilt that was still warm to the touch.

"No!" I cried.

I ran to my room with the horrible quilt clutched in my hand and got a pair of scissors. I was ready to cut the thing into a million pieces. But as I brought the scissors to the fabric I knew that I couldn't do it—because of something I saw *inside* the quilt.

There, at the very corner of the fabric, was a new patchwork square. Two ovals of tan velvet on a purple cotton background. And, when I looked at it hard enough, those ovals became two faces—*their* faces. I could see my brother's and my sister's eyes, just like all the other eyes, silently staring out at me from inside the quilt.

The following Saturday, Mom and Dad had a garage sale.

"Look at this!" said a woman who rummaged through the piles of children's clothes and children's toys. "It's a double stroller!" She was talking to her husband, who held newborn twins in his arms. "Just what we need," the woman went on, and then she turned to my mother. "I guess your twins have outgrown it," she said, giving the stroller a friendly pat.

My mother just stared at her, blinking. "No, we don't have twins," she said.

The woman glanced around at the piles of clothes. "But you seem to have two of everything, so I thought—"

"The stroller was in the garage," my mother said with a shrug. "I don't know how it got there . . . maybe it was from the previous owner."

And then Mom walked off to help some other customers. I almost said something, but what good would it do? I was the only one who remembered the twins. To everyone else, it was as though they had never existed.

"You're lucky," said my friend Corinne, who was rummaging through our stuff as well. "You're lucky you're an only child. I have to share everything with my little brother."

And then Corinne picked up the many-colored quilt, which lay folded across a plastic teeter-totter.

"I should give this to my brother to replace that disgusting old security blanket he carries around the house," said Corinne. "How much do you want for it?"

I thought about it. I thought about it a long time. And in the end I let her have it.

"Take it," I told her. "It's free."

And why not? Who was I to stop the quilt on its journey through this world? And besides . . . misery loves company.

GROWING PAINS

THE SCREAM STABBED INTO CODY FENCHURCH'S SLEEP,
tearing a jagged hole in his dream. He had been dreaming he
was tall—the tallest kid in school—towering over all the
other kids who always teased him about his height. But great
dreams like that never last, and Cody was dragged away from
that happy fantasy, into the cold darkness of his room. He
sat up, blinking in the moonlight, wondering who had
screamed—and why.

Suddenly a second scream rattled his half-opened window, and Cody knew that both screams had come from next
door. That's where his best friend, Warren Burke, lived.

Cody stared through his large window and could see
right into Warren's room. He could see his friend sitting in
bed and wailing. What was happening in there? It sounded
like Warren was being torn to pieces.

Cody watched as the lights came on next door, and
Warren's parents raced into his room. By then, Warren was
running around, waving and thrashing his arms at empty air.

Soon Cody realized that his own parents were awake,

too. He heard them whispering down the hall, talking about what was going on at the neighbor's house, and wondering what to do. Then his dad poked his head into Cody's room. "You okay, sport?" he asked.

Cody assured his dad that he was, then he tried to go back to sleep. That's when Warren screamed again, and this time Cody heard him say something, too.

"Don't let them come back!" Warren shrieked. "Don't let them take me again! It's horrible! Horrible!"

Cody listened to Warren's mad ravings, and then he listened to Mr. and Mrs. Burke trying to calm him down. "It's only a dream," they kept telling him over and over again.

But that didn't seem to calm Warren down in the least. In fact, he continued to scream the rest of that awful, endless night, and Cody slept—or tried to sleep—with a pillow over his head.

In the morning, Warren was still screaming. And he was still screaming that next afternoon . . . when he was taken off to the hospital. As far as Cody knew, Warren never did stop screaming.

And that's how Cody Fenchurch lost his best friend.

"But you have to try to sleep," Cody's mom insisted. It had been three weeks since Warren Burke had been taken away, and once again, here Cody was, lying on his bed, his eyes wide open.

"You know what they say," his mother offered. "You grow when you sleep."

"I'm trying," said Cody, rolling over restlessly. "I always try."

His mother raised an eyebrow. "You're thinking about Warren, aren't you?"

"No," Cody said flatly. It was a lie, of course. How could he not think about Warren? He thought about him every time he looked out his window and saw his friend's empty room across the way. He thought about him every time he walked home from school—alone.

"Would you like to visit Warren?" Cody's mom asked.

Cody sat up in bed. "You mean they let kids visit other kids in the asylum?"

She wrinkled her nose, as if the word *asylum* had a stench to it. "They don't call those places asylums anymore, Cody," she informed him. "They're just hospitals—*special* hospitals."

Cody thought about that and looked out the window toward Warren's dark, empty room. For years he and Warren had talked to each other at night across the narrow pathway between their two houses, about all sorts of things—school, girls, sports—and growing up.

Growing up.

That had been a sore point with Cody. He and Warren had always been about the same height until fifth grade. But then Warren had started having what they called "growth spurts." One summer he even grew two whole inches.

But Cody didn't have any growth spurts. In fact, he hadn't grown a fraction of an inch in two years. While all the other kids in school were sprouting long, clumsy arms and legs, Cody remained unchanged.

Now, in the middle of seventh grade, Cody was the shortest kid in the class, and Warren, if he hadn't been locked away somewhere, would have been the tallest. Cody remembered how ridiculous he used to feel walking home next to Warren. But Warren had never made fun of Cody's size—not like the other kids. That's why they had been able to stay best friends.

So now that his best friend went insane and was taken away, did Cody want to visit him? Did he *really* want to visit Warren after he had seen him scream for twelve straight hours?

Cody looked at his mom, who was standing at the edge of his bed. "Is it true that Warren's hair turned white that night?" he blurted out.

His mother offered him a slim smile and said wistfully, "That happens sometimes."

Harmony Home for Children did its best to be pleasant and inviting, but the disinfectant-scented linoleum couldn't hide the smell of decay, and the music pumped into the air couldn't hide the sounds of madness.

Warren was in a room at the end of a long hallway papered with balloons and teddy bears. It was the type of wallpaper that would have made Warren gag in his old, real life, Cody mused as he stepped into the barely furnished room with his mother. A nurse, who was required to stay during all visits, sat in the corner.

All that was in the room was a bed, a dresser with baby-proof latches, and Warren, crouched in his bed, staring at the wall across from him. He cowered as if there were a monster across the room, but there was nothing there but the same balloons and teddy bears that had invaded the hall.

The nurse smiled, as if it were her job to smile. "Stimulation is important for Warren," she said. "He needs to know that people still remember him—that his old life is still out there when he's ready to go back to it."

Cody cleared his throat and held on to his mother like a small child. "What's up, Warren?" he asked.

But Warren didn't turn to look at him. Instead he just hummed to himself.

Cody tentatively let go of the death-grip he had on his mother's arm and took a few steps closer.

Warren still didn't look at him, but he did speak.

"They let you in here?" he asked. "Why did they let you in here?"

Warren's voice sounded empty and far away. Cody noticed that his hair wasn't quite white but ashen gray, standing on end, and hopelessly tangled. This was not the Warren Burke that Cody knew.

"Yeah, sure, they let me in," Cody said, offering a lopsided smile. "You doin' okay?"

Warren shook his head and backed farther into the corner of his bed as Cody approached. "Don't let them get you!" he shrieked, his voice a wild warble. "Stay awake all night! Run when you see them coming! Don't let them take you to that place."

Cody could feel his own hair start to stand on end, but he had to ask. "Who? Who's going to get me? And where am I supposed to keep them from taking me?"

Warren could only stare at Cody in horror.

The nurse, who didn't seem pleased with the direction of the conversation, pulled open the curtains. "Maybe we could all take a look at the view," she said. And then she turned to Warren. "Why don't you tell your little friend all about the walks we've been taking around the lake, Warren?

Tell him how they help your nerves."

Cody looked out the window. The view might have been beautiful elsewhere, but not for the people here. The bars on the window could never let them forget where they were.

But Warren didn't seem interested in the view anyway. He just kept staring over at the wall as if waiting for something to happen.

Suddenly Cody's mother, who had been sitting quietly by the door, turned to the nurse and asked, "Is Warren getting any . . . better?"

"Oh, yes!" chimed the nurse, as if it were her job to chime. "He's growing stronger every day!"

"Growing!" said Warren, with a sneer in his voice. Then he snapped his eyes to Cody. "You're lucky," he said. "You're lucky you're so small. Growing as fast as I did was the worst thing that ever happened to me!"

"Now, Warren," said the nurse in her practiced, soothing voice. "Remember, we have to think positive thoughts." And she cast her eyes down to the little paper cup on the dresser to make sure he had taken his medication.

"I'll never have a positive thought again," said Warren. "Not after what I saw—not after what I *felt*."

Cody couldn't resist. "What did you feel?" he asked.

Warren's eyes went wide and his lips stretched back in a grimace, as if he were feeling it all over again.

"Growing pains," he hissed.

The nurse was beginning to act a little nervous. "Warren, why don't you take your little friend out to the rec room," she suggested. "You could play Ping-Pong, or a nice game of Scrabble."

But Warren wasn't interested in games. He reached

out, grabbed Cody by the shirt, and pulled him close.

"We grow when we sleep . . ." Warren whispered desperately in Cody's ear. And then, out of nowhere, he began to scream the way he had that first night—emptying his lungs, then gasping for air, and emptying his lungs over and over again.

Cody turned and ran, bursting out the door and racing down the long hallway. He didn't stop until he was outside, where Warren's screams blended in with the screams of all the other children who had gone mad.

A few days later, with the memory of the hospital still fresh in his mind, Cody visited the auto shop where his father worked. It was a restless place, where exhausted mechanics created automotive wonders. There were engines torn apart into a thousand small greasy pieces that would somehow fit together like a jigsaw puzzle. There were whole cars gutted to make room for bigger engines that nature never intended. But strangest of all was the department his father managed, where they took big Cadillacs and made them even bigger.

As Cody stepped into the shop, his father was supervising one such procedure. A blue sedan, already stripped of its doors, was practically being sawed in half because the owner wanted five more feet of legroom. But today Cody hadn't come to watch them build a limo. He had come to talk to his dad.

"Did you ever know anyone who . . . uh, snapped . . . the way Warren did?" Cody asked when he had finally gotten his father alone in his small office.

"No," his father replied, but he had hesitated long

enough for Cody to know that he was lying. His dad walked over and closed the door of his office, muffling the noise of the shop. Then he looked Cody straight in the eyes.

"Don't tell your mother I told you this," he said, "or she'll blame me for giving you nightmares." He cleared his throat and began to pace. "I had this friend once, when I was about your age. Anyway, he went nuts, kind of the way Warren did. I wasn't there, but I heard about it—*everyone* heard about it, and there were lots of rumors."

He paused for a moment, then went on. "Some people said my friend got hit in the head too hard—his dad was a mean son-of-a-gun. Others said he was never right in the head to begin with. Anyway, the story his parents gave was that he woke up screaming in the middle of the night, saying that the angels had come to take him. He kept on screaming, so they sent him away, and no one ever heard from him again."

"What do you think happened to your friend that night, Dad?" Cody asked.

His father scratched his neck and shrugged. "Probably nothing," he said. "And as for the things he said—well, it was just something made up by a mind that was about to go crazy . . . or already had."

Cody squirmed and felt his skin begin to crawl. "Maybe what happened to your friend is what happened to Warren," he suggested. "You see, after I ran out of Warren's room at the hospital, I sat out there on the porch of that Harmony Home place where they're keeping him, and I heard other kids screaming, too. I couldn't tell for sure, but they all seemed to be screaming about something that came in the middle of the night to take them away. Angels . . .

monsters . . . aliens . . . whatever."

Cody's Dad looked at him for a moment, and then laughed, slapping him on the back. "You sure have some imagination," he said. "Not bad for a little guy."

Cody gave him a cold stare. "I'm not so little."

"Oh, don't be so sensitive," said his dad. "You'll grow soon—I can feel it in my bones."

They came at three in the morning.

It had been another sleepless night for Cody. He had counted about a thousand sheep and still hadn't so much as drifted off. He was about to start counting a new, larger flock of sheep . . . when they came. It began as a breeze he felt on the tip of his nose—but he remembered that his window was closed. Cody snapped his eyes open and looked across to the opposite wall.

A line had appeared—a thin black line—and it ran from ceiling to floor, spreading like a fissure or some kind of hole in space. Then, hands started to reach out of the hole—dozens of hands. And then, suddenly, there were people in the room! Cody tried to scream, but one large, heavy hand, cold and antiseptic-smelling, covered his mouth. Then several others grabbed Cody's arms and legs. He struggled wildly, but the hands were strong, and with little effort, they dragged him toward the hole, drawing him through the cold, dark fissure and into a bright white light.

All at once Cody felt himself being lifted onto something . . . then he was rolling, flat on his back, and suddenly he knew he was in . . . a hospital.

He was strapped down to a gurney and being rolled

through clean white hallways. He kept his eyes fixed on a man with a clipboard, running alongside him. The man was clean-cut, clean-shaven, and had spotless white teeth.

"I'm Farnsworth, public relations," said the man with a perfect smile. "It's good to see you again, Cody. It's been a while."

"I've never seen you before!" wailed Cody, fighting to get free from the tight bonds around him.

"Of course you have," said Farnsworth reassuringly. "You just don't remember."

"Take me back home!"

"In time, Cody."

The four hospital workers who had pulled him out of bed and through the hole in space now wheeled him down the impossibly long hallway like pallbearers with a casket. Farnsworth jogged alongside, making sure that everything went smoothly.

"Are you . . . an angel?" asked Cody.

Farnsworth laughed. "Heavens, no," he said. "None of us are. We're just the medical staff."

Farnsworth looked at his clipboard. "Things have been busy around here lately," he said. "We're backed up—almost a year behind—and you're way overdue."

"F-for what?" Cody stammered.

"A growth spurt, of course," answered Farnsworth.

They pushed Cody through a set of double doors and into a huge room that seemed to be the size of a stadium.

"Welcome to the Growth Ward!" Farnsworth announced.

In the room were thousands of surgeons, huddled together over patients . . . all of whom were kids.

Cody couldn't believe what he was seeing. It was like

his father's auto shop, but instead of cars it was kids being taken apart and being put back together again—piece by piece. But what was most amazing of all was that these kids, in various stages of repair, were all alive!

And they were also awake.

Some screamed, others just groaned, and the ones who no longer had the strength to even groan just watched in terror as the "medical staff" dismantled them, then rebuilt them before their own horrified eyes.

"What are you doing to them?" shouted Cody. "What's going on here?"

"Body work and scheduled maintenance, of course," said Farnsworth over the awful wails around him. "How can a person be expected to grow without their maintenance appointments?"

"You're killing them!" yelled Cody.

"Nonsense, our surgeons are the most skilled in the universe," said Farnsworth cheerfully. "These kids will be patched up and back to their old selves by morning—and without a single scar from the experience."

"But I don't need surgery. I don't WANT surgery," Cody insisted.

"Why should you be different from everyone else?" asked Farnsworth. "And besides, you *do* want it." He smiled. "You do want to grow, don't you?"

Cody felt weak and sick to his stomach. "You mean . . . *this* happens to everybody?"

"Of course it does," explained Farnsworth. "Nobody remembers, though, because we erase it from their memory." Then the smile left Farnsworth's face, and he shook his head sadly. "Of course, every once in a while the memory-erasing doesn't quite work. It's a shame, really—those poor kids are ruined for life, and all because they couldn't forget the Growth Ward."

Cody was still trying to digest what Farnsworth had just said, when he was rolled into a bright area where a group of surgeons waited. Their faces covered with masks, they anxiously flexed their fingers like pianists preparing for a concert. As Cody stared in horror at them, he noticed that there was something about those surgeons—something not quite right, but what was it? Keeping his eyes glued on them, Cody knew if he looked at them long enough, he'd figure out what it was that made them look . . . different.

"It says here, we're adding half an inch to your fore-arms today," Farnsworth said, glancing at his clipboard again. "And a whole inch to your thigh-bones. Good for you, Cody! We'll have you caught up to those other kids in your class in no time!"

Cody turned to see a silver tray next to the operating table. On it were a few small, circular bone fragments, no larger than Lego pieces.

One of the eager surgeons grabbed a small bone saw from the tray and turned it on. It buzzed and whined, adding to the many unpleasant sounds of the great galactic operating room.

The surgeon said nothing and moved the saw toward Cody's leg, and the others approached him with their scalpels poised.

"No!" Cody cried. "You can't operate without anesthesia! I have to have anesthesia!"

Farnsworth chuckled. "Come now, Cody, where do you think you are, at the dentist? I think not! Growing pains are a part of life, and *everyone* has to feel their growing pains. *Everyone*."

Cody screamed even before the instruments touched his body—then he suddenly realized that it didn't matter how loud he wailed. For he had finally figured out what was wrong with those surgeons. They couldn't hear him. They had no ears.

I need to remember . . .

    I need to remember . . .

    I need to remember . . . what?

An alarm tore Cody out of the deepest sleep he had ever had. There was a memory of a dream—or something like a dream—but it was quickly fading into darkness. In a moment it was completely gone, and all that was left was the light of day pouring into his room.

"Wake up, lazy bones," said his mother. "You'll be late for school."

Cody felt good this morning. No—*better* than good— he felt great, and he couldn't quite tell why. He stood up out of bed and felt a slight case of vertigo, as if the floor were somehow farther away from him than it had been the day before. His legs and arms ached the slightest bit, but that was okay. It was a *good* feeling.

"My, how you're growing!" his mother said as he walked into the kitchen for breakfast. "I'll bet you'll grow three inches by fall!"

And the thought made Cody smile. It felt good to be a growing boy.

CONNECTING FLIGHT

THE NARROW, DOORLESS HALL SEEMS TO STRETCH ON forever.

The bag slung across her shoulder seems full of lead.

And the image of her parents waving good-bye still sticks in her mind.

With a boarding pass in hand, Jana Martinez walks down a narrow, tilted corridor, toward the 737 at the end of the Jetway.

She tries to forget the strange state of cold limbo that fills the gap between her parents behind her and her final destination—Wendingham Prep School.

It is only three hours away now—just a two-hour flight from Chicago to Boston, and then an hour's bus ride. Still, to Jana, this empty time between two places always seems to last an eternity.

She reaches the door of the plane, stumbling over the lip of the hatch, and a flight attendant grabs her arm too tightly. "Watch your step," the flight attendant says, trying to help Jana keep her balance.

Now, as she makes her way down the narrow aisle, Jana wonders if the flight attendant's overly-strong grip will leave a bruise on her arm. She is sure the cruel strap of her carry-on bag will leave her black and blue.

The plane is divided by a single center aisle, and each row has three seats on either side. Jana finds her seat by the window on the left side of the plane. She has to climb over a heavy, pale woman to get there, and just as she finally settles in, her sense of loneliness settles in deeper than before.

I'm surrounded by strangers, she thinks. *I'm unknown to all of them . . . and unconnected.*

The plane is filled with people she's never seen before and will never see again—filled with hundreds of lives that intersect nowhere but on this plane. The feeling is eerie to Jana, and unnatural.

The woman beside her is several sizes too large for the seat, and her large body spreads toward Jana, taking over Jana's armrest, and forcing her to lean uncomfortably against the cold window.

"Sorry, dearie," says the woman, with a British accent. "You'd think people have no hips, the way they build these seats."

The woman also has bad breath.

Jana sighs, calculates how many seconds there are in a two-hour flight, and begins to count down from seven-thousand-two-hundred. She wonders if a flight could possibly be any worse. Soon she finds out that it can.

A woman with a baby takes the seat next to the large English woman, and the moment the plane leaves the ground, the baby begins an ear-splitting screech-fest. The mother tries to console the child, but it does no good.

Grimacing, Jana notices an old man sitting across the aisle turn down his hearing aid.

"Why do I always end up on Screaming Baby Airlines?" Jana grumbles to herself, and the large woman in her airspace accidentally overhears. She turns to Jana with a smile.

"It's the pressure in its ears, the poor thing," says the large woman, pointing to the wailing baby. Then she adds something curious. "Babies on planes comfort me, actually. I always think, God won't crash a plane carrying a baby."

The thought that seems to give so much comfort to the large woman only gives Jana the creeps. She peers out her window, watching as the plane rises above little puffs of clouds that soon look like tiny white specks far below.

"We've reached our cruising altitude of 35,000 feet, and *blah, blah, blah,*" drones the captain, who seems to have the same voice as every other airline pilot in the world. It's as if they go to some special school that teaches them all how to sound exactly alike.

The baby, having exhausted its screaming machine, can only whimper now, and the plump woman, who has introduced herself as Moira Lester, turns to Jana and asks, "You'll be visiting someone in Boston, then?"

"School," says Jana curtly, not feeling like having a conversation with a stranger.

"Boarding school, is it?" asks Moira, not taking the hint. "I went to boarding school. It's all the rage back in Britain. Not many of them in the States, are there?" And then she begins to spin the never-ending tale of her uninteresting family, all the boarding schools they attended, why they went there, and which classmates have become famous people that Jana has never heard of.

Jana nods as if listening but tries to tune her out by gazing out the window at the specks of clouds below. It is just about then that the feeling comes. It's a sensation—a *twinge*, like a spark of static electricity darting through her, that causes a tiny, tiny change in air pressure. It's like a pinprick in her reality—a feeling so slight that it takes a while for Jana to realize that she has felt anything at all.

As she turns from the window to look around her, nothing appears to have changed: Moira is still talking, the baby is still whimpering.

But as for Jana, she has a clear sense that something is suddenly not right.

"Something wrong, dearie?" Moira asks.

But Jana just shakes her head, trying to convince herself that it's only her imagination.

Then, about ten minutes later, Jana asks, "Where's the old man?" The sense of something wrong had been growing and growing within her, and now, she has finally noticed something different.

The mother, bouncing her baby on her knee, looks at Jana oddly. "What old man?" she asks.

"You know—the old man who was sitting across the aisle from you. He was wearing a hearing aid."

The mother turns to look. Sitting across the aisle is a businessman with slick black hair. Certainly not old, and definitely not wearing a hearing aid, he sits reading a magazine in seat 16-D as if he belongs there.

"Don't you remember him?" Jana persists. "He turned down his hearing aid when your baby was screaming."

The mother shrugs. "I didn't notice," she says. "Who notices anybody on airplanes these days?"

"Looks like there are some empty seats on the plane," suggests Moira. "Perhaps this man you're talking about moved."

Jana sighs. "Yeah, maybe that's it," she concedes, although not really convinced. She would have noticed if the man had gotten up.

"Excuse me," Jana says and climbs over Moira and the mother and her baby, then heads down the aisle to the bathroom. There is something wrong, she knows it. Something terribly wrong. She can feel it in the pit of her stomach, like the feeling you get a few minutes before becoming violently ill.

Jana pushes her way through the narrow bathroom doorway and into the tight little compartment. Jana looks in the mirror, then splashes cold water on her face. *Maybe it's just the excitement of going back to school*, she tells herself. *Maybe it's just airsickness*.

But where is that man with the hearing aid?

She dries her face with a paper towel and makes her way back to her seat, looking in every row for the old man. She goes to the very front of the plane. No old man with a hearing aid. What did he do? Jump off the plane?

When Jana returns to her seat, the mother and baby have moved to where she can lay her baby down on an empty seat—a few rows back on the other side of the plane. As Jana looks around, she notices that there are empty seats, and even empty rows on the plane now—but all the vacant seats appear to be on the side of the plane opposite her.

Jana stands there watching as several people from her side of the plane shift over to make use of the empty rows, making more room for everyone. How odd—the plane seemed crowded when she got on.

When Jana retakes her seat, Moira welcomes her back with a wide friendly smile. Jana forces her own smile, and as she settles in, she happens to glance out the window . . . then freezes.

"Moira," she says, "everything's covered in clouds!"

Moira glances out the window at the cotton-thick clouds rolling toward the horizon below. "Why, I suppose it is," she says.

"Excuse me," Jana says as she climbs back over Moira and crosses the aisle. She then leans awkwardly over the businessman and two other passengers to get a look out *their* window. She is certain she hadn't seen clouds out of the other side of the plane on her way back from the bathroom.

Sure enough, from this window, Jana can see the ground—a patchwork quilt of greens and browns gilded by the afternoon sun.

"It—it's *different* on this side of the plane," she observes, her voice shaky.

"So what?" asks the businessman, annoyed at the way Jana is still leaning across him. "We must be traveling along the edge of a front. You know—the line where cold air meets warm air, and storm clouds form."

Jana just stares at him, feeling her hands growing colder by the moment. *It's a logical explanation*, she thinks, *but it's wrong.*

Quietly Jana returns to her seat. She pulls out the magazine in the pouch in front of her and tries to read it, but finds nothing can take her attention away from the clouds beneath her window, and the perfectly clear sky on the other side of the plane.

That's when the captain comes on the loudspeaker again.

"Just thought I'd let you know," he says in his every-pilot voice, "that we'll be passing Mount Rushmore shortly. If you look out the right side of the plane, you'll be able to see it on the horizon."

Jana doesn't bother to look, since she's on the left side. But she does notice that people on her side of the plane are chuckling, as if the pilot has made some kind of joke.

Then it hits her.

Geography was never one of Jana's best subjects, but she's sure that Mount Rushmore is not in Ohio—the state they should have been over right now! She turns to Moira. "Where is Mount Rushmore?" she asks, trying not to sound panicked.

"Can't say for sure," the heavyset woman replies. "I haven't been in the States long."

"This *is* the flight to Boston, isn't it?"

"As far as I know," says Moira. "At least that's what my ticket says."

Jana uneasily mulls over everything as she goes back to staring out her window . . . at nothing but clouds.

About an hour and a half into the flight, Jana has bitten her nails down to stubs—a habit she thought she had broken years ago. That tiny tear in the fabric of her safe and sane world that happened a while back has shred so rapidly, Jana wonders if it can ever be sewn back together again.

It is now dark outside her window. Jana reasons that that is perfectly normal. She has flown enough to know that when flying east at dusk, the sun always sets behind you incredibly fast. It has to do with the curvature of the earth, and time zones, and that sort of thing. Perfectly natural . . . except that the sun is still shining on the other side of the plane.

The plane is filled with anxious murmurs. Perhaps Jana was the first one to realize things were screwy, but now everyone sees it.

"There's some explanation," one person whispers.

"We'll probably all laugh about it later," another says.

And indeed, some people are laughing already, as if laughing could make it all better.

Sitting there, with no nails left to bite, Jana wonders if it is always like this when things go wrong in midair. Do people not scream and wail the way they do in the movies? Do they get quiet . . . like this . . or just whisper, or laugh? And if they do scream, do they only scream on the inside?

Jana calls the flight attendant over.

"Excuse me," she says, her voice quivering with panic, "but we have to land this plane. We have to land it *now!*"

The flight attendant smiles and speaks with practiced reassurance, as if Jana is nothing more than an anxious flier. "We've begun our final descent," she tells her. "We should be on the ground shortly."

"Haven't you looked out the window?" Jana snaps at the flight attendant. "Haven't you seen what's happening out there?"

"Weather conditions up here," says the flight attendant, "aren't like weather conditions on the ground."

"Night and day aren't weather conditions!" shouts Jana. The nervous murmurs can now be heard around the cabin.

The flight attendant looks into Jana's eyes, grits her teeth furiously, and says, "I'll have to ask you to sit down, miss."

That look on the flight attendant's face says everything. It says, *We have no idea what's going on, but we can't admit that, you stupid girl! If we do, everyone will start panicking. So shut your face before we shut it for you!*

The flight attendant storms away, and Jana dares to do something she's been wanting to do since the sky began to change. She looks across the aisle to the businessman and asks him where he's going.

"Seattle," he says. "I'm going to Seattle—of course—just like you."

Several people on Jana's side of the plane gasp and whisper to one another, as if being quiet about it makes the situation any less horrific than it is.

"I thought this flight was going to Boston," says Moira.

"She's right," says another passenger behind Moira. "This plane is going to Boston."

The businessman swallows. "There must be some sort of . . . computer mix-up."

Jana sinks in her seat as the plane passes through the heavy cloud cover—on *her* side of the plane—and as soon as they punch though the clouds, she can see the twinkling lights of a city below. She doesn't dare look out the windows on the other side of the plane anymore.

In Seattle, Jana thinks, *it would still be light out.*

The truth was simple, and at the same time impossible to comprehend. Somehow, some grand computer glitch—not in any simple airline computer—got two flights . . . confused.

A flight like this will never reach the ground, she tells herself. *How can it?*

Suddenly the plane shudders and whines as the landing

gear doors open. People are all looking out their windows at the night on the left side of the plane, and then at the day on the right. Slowly cold terror paints their faces a pale white.

Across the aisle and three rows back, the baby screams again as they descend. To Jana, the screams are far less disturbing than the whispers and silences of all the other passengers, but not to everyone.

"Shut that child up!" shouts the businessman.

But the mother can do nothing but hold her baby close to her as they sit across the narrow aisle, waiting for the plane to touch down.

Across the aisle? Jana's mind suddenly screams. And then that sickening feeling that began almost two hours ago spreads through her arms and legs, until every part of her body feels weak. Jana glances at the empty seat right next to Moira and erupts with panic. She opens her seat belt, stands and shouts to the mother, yelling louder than the woman's screaming baby.

"Get up!" Jana shouts "You have to come back to this seat!"

"But we're landing," says the mother nervously. "I shouldn't unbuckle my seat belt."

"You're not *supposed* to be there!" Jana insists. "You started on *this* side. I can't explain it now—but you have to come back to this side of the plane—NOW!"

Terrified, the mother unbuckles her seat belt and, clutching her screaming baby, crosses the aisle the moment the tires touch the runway. Others who had moved to the empty seats on the right side sense what is about to happen. They race to get out of their seat belts and back to their original seats—but they are not fast enough.

In an instant, there is a burst of flame, and the world seems to end.

"Help me!" screams the mother.

Jana grabs the woman's hand, while Moira grabs the baby. They fall into the seat next to Moira, and the mother shields her baby from the nightmare exploding around them.

Everyone screams as the plane spins and tumbles out of control—everyone but Jana. She glances out her window to see that nothing seems wrong. The plane is landing in Boston, just like planes always land.

But on the other side of the plane, the *right* side of the plane, there is smoke and flames and shredding steel. And, beyond the shattering windows, the ground is rolling over and over. In awe, Jana watches as the smoke billows . . . but *stays* on the other side of the aisle. In fact, Jana can't even smell it!

Moira leans into Jana. "Don't look!" she cries. "You mustn't look at it!"

And Jana knows that Moira is right. So instead, she holds Moira's hand and turns to look out her own window. Tears rolling down her cheeks, she watches the terminal roll peacefully toward her. She feels the plane calmly slow down, and she tries to ignore the awful wails from the other side of the plane . . . until the last wail trails off.

Then the captain begins to speak, uncertain at first, but then with building confidence. "Uh . . . on behalf of our crew, I'd like to welcome you to . . . Boston. Please remain seated until we are secure at the terminal."

The screaming has stopped. The only sound now is that of the engines powering down to a low whine. Slowly Jana dares to look across the aisle.

There, she finds the man with the hearing aid staring back at her, aghast.

On the other side of the plane are all the people who had been there when they had taken off. Now that Jana sees their faces, she can recognize them.

Someone must have fixed the computer, Jana thinks, and then she turns to Moira. "Do you suppose that while we were watching the right half of that flight to Seattle—"

"—that the people on the other side were watching the left half?" finishes Moira. "Look at their faces. I can only imagine that they were."

The mother, whose baby has stopped screaming and has fallen asleep, thanks Jana with tears in her eyes. Jana touches the baby's fine hair, then smiles. Suddenly it seems that all those long stories Moira has told on the plane don't seem so boring, and in a way Jana longs to hear all of them again. In fact, she longs to hear every story of every person on that plane. *There are so many lives intersecting on an airplane,* she thinks. *So many stories to hear!*

Jana walks with Moira to the baggage claim, where suitcases are already flying down the chute and circling on the baggage carousel. There, Jana watches people from her flight greet friends and family who have been waiting for them.

"I just heard that a flight out west didn't make it," someone says. "It was the same airline, too."

But no one from Jana's flight says anything. How can you tell someone that you saw a plane crash from the inside, but it wasn't *your* plane?

"It's good that things ended up back where they belong," Moira says.

"There's nothing 'good,' about it," says Jana flatly.

"No, I suppose not," Moira agrees. "But it's right. Right and proper."

Together, Jana and Moira wait a long time for their luggage, but it never comes. Jana has to admit that she didn't expect it to.

Not when all the luggage coming down the chute is ticketed to Seattle.

CRYSTALLOID

THE SAND-TRAP HAD ALREADY CLAIMED A NEIGHBOR'S dog. At least that was the rumor. They said the poor animal had gone down slowly, like it had been sucked into quicksand. It must have felt the same way a dinosaur felt when it got stuck in a tar pit and sank inch by inch into hot, black eternity.

Of course, nobody believed the rumor. Quicksand? On a beach? No such thing! No, that stuff was only in the Amazon or deep in the Congo—and anyone foolish enough to poke around in places like that deserved whatever they got.

But I believed it. People didn't make up things like that—not unless they were particularly twisted. That's what made me trek down that long strip of empty beach near my grandma's old beach house. I had to check it out for myself.

I'd been living with Grandma almost four months now. It was my dad's new girlfriend's idea, and at first, I was just supposed to spend the summer.

"It's for Philip's own good," she had said, sounding so caring, as if the real reason she wanted to get rid of me had anything to do with helping me. Anyway, she convinced my dad it was a last-ditch effort to keep me out of trouble. After all, ever since my dad and mom split, I had developed a special talent for getting rid of his girlfriends. Maybe my dad figured if I were out of the picture, that wouldn't happen anymore.

Anyway, it worked. They spent the summer together in Europe, and I kept out of trouble—if you don't count that first day, when I got mad and shattered a bunch of glass figurines in Grandma's crafts shop.

In fact, I've done so well out here, my dad and his girlfriend decided to leave me in this lonely part of the world for good. Or at least it seems that way.

So, since it looks like I don't have a choice, I've been trying to make the best of it, and I've actually grown to like these desolate beaches better than the crowded city I used to live in. Of course, the kids at school out here are kind of time-warped back a dozen years or so. But I can put up with that. After all, I have little mysteries to spice up my day— like pets disappearing in the Sand-Trap.

The rumor about the dog had been going around school for a day or two before I actually decided to check it out. It was early on a Saturday morning, and as I left the house, a wall of storm clouds had stalled on the horizon. They seemed to be taunting the little beach community, sounding off dull thunder every now and then, but keeping their distance, like an army waiting to attack.

"You have no business going out on a day like this," Grandma warned me. "The wind'll blow you halfway to tomorrow."

Of course that didn't stop me. Weather never did. And

neither did warnings. Besides, I loved going out when it was cold and windy. I didn't tell Grandma where I was going, though—that I was going to the Sand-Trap, and that I was taking a bucket with me.

As I trudged along the smooth shoreline, I breathed in the ocean spray that chilled me inside and out, then I opened my shirt and let the cold of the day fill my body with goose bumps. People didn't understand why I liked to feel cold all the time. I couldn't explain it, either.

A few hundred yards down the strand, I finally came to the weird, perfectly-round patch of sand on the beach behind Grandma's house. Everyone called it the Sand-Trap because it was always a few inches lower, and a few shades lighter than all the other sand around it. But what was really weird was that the Sand-Trap washed away every day in high tide, then always came back to reform itself—once again, perfectly round. And, when you looked down at it long enough, you could swear the sand was moving. But that was just an optical illusion—I was sure of it.

I stood before the Sand-Trap for the longest time, building up my nerve to do what I had decided to do . . . and then I stepped into it.

Instantly I noticed that this sand was finer than the rest of the sand on the beach—and it was colder, too. But was it quicksand? I didn't think so, after all, I didn't start sinking.

And so I got down on my knees in the Sand-Trap, and I stared into it until I could see the sand slowly start churning. Then I dug my hands into it and filled my bucket to the brim. I had wanted some of that strange sand ever since I heard it existed, and now, at last, I was going to have some of it for my very own.

The windows in Grandma's workshop were always wide open because of the heat from the furnace and blowtorch. You see, Grandma was a glassblower. She created bowls and jars and dainty little crystalline figurines that she sold in a crafts shop right next to her house.

That first day, after I had smashed that shelf of figurines, Grandma, instead of yelling at me, sat me down and showed me exactly how much work it took to make just one of the delicate pieces. She also told me how good Grandpa had been at it. "He had always wanted to teach you," she told me, a bit of sadness in her voice, "but you never had the interest."

But after living with Grandma for a while and watching her work the glass, I did develop an interest. There was something about the molten glass that fascinated me, and I grew to love learning the craft.

At first, all I could make were lopsided glasses and mystery ashtrays—everything with sides that didn't quite stay up was a mystery ashtray. But that was three months ago. I've gotten much better at glassblowing now, and I spend most of my free time in that workshop making things.

The things I make aren't cute little animals, though. Mine are powerful beasts. Tigers with angry eyes. Dragons breathing crystalline fire. Glass sharks with bloody teeth. Grandma sells them in the shop, too. She even gave me my own shelf to display my creatures, and she labeled my shelf "Phantastic Phenomena by Philip."

Now, Grandma never knows what to make of my creations, and she just eyes them with a look that's half proud and half worried. "I guess it's better to get your monsters out of you, than to keep them inside," she told me once, laughing nervously.

"Well, there are lots more where those came from," I wanted to tell her. And then I thought of the Sand-Trap sand and said nothing. As far as I knew nobody had ever blown a glass creature from *that* sand.

As soon as I had dragged the bucket of strange sand back to the workshop, I began to work with it. First, with the fire turned full blast, I quickly melted the sand into a thick semiliquid. Next I wrapped it around my glassblowing pipe. It wasn't muddy and speckled like other unpurified glass, but instead it burned a clean white-hot. Then I held out the stick and watched as it dripped down the stick, inching toward my fingers like the *Blob*.

"You will be incredible!" I told it. "You will be like nothing I've created before." And with that, I put my lips to the end of the tube and blew into the pulsating mass of hot liquid glass.

Grandma almost screamed when she saw it later that week. Her face went white, and at first I thought she was going to pass out. Then I realized she was just stunned by my creation. I grinned, entirely pleased with myself.

"Do you like it?" I asked.

She caught her breath. "Philip . . . I don't know what to say." She dared to venture closer. "Is this what you've been working on all week?"

"Pretty cool, huh?"

Grandma grimaced. "Well, it sure is something . . . I just don't know what."

To me, it was everything I imagined it would be. The glass creature stood there capturing the late afternoon sun, sending out daggers of light in all directions. Two feet tall, with claws that were sharp and menacing, it had shiny muscles on its hind legs that bulged, looking as though they were ready to pounce. When you looked at it long enough, you would swear you could see it moving.

Its animalistic face was like nothing on earth that I'd ever seen. It had a long snout, and a menacing grin filled with row after row of razor-sharp teeth. Its nostrils flared; its large eyes seemed to follow you around the room. The thing could scare a gargoyle right off its foundation.

"My masterpiece!" I told Grandma.

"Uh, maybe you've been spending too much time blowing glass," she suggested. Then she left to make dinner, and I closed up the shop—which gave me more time to admire my creation.

"You need a name," I told my crystalline beast as it sat there on a wooden countertop, for it was too large to fit on my display shelf. I thought and I thought, but no name I came up with seemed right. "Perhaps you're something best left nameless, huh?"

Outside I could hear a chill wind blowing, sending shivers up my spine . . . just the way I liked it.

I awoke the next morning to the storm that had been looming offshore for days, and was now finally rolling in with a vengeance. I slept with the window open so the sill and the carpet beneath it were drenched. My toes and fingertips had grown hard from the cold, the numbness inching up through the rest of my body, which shivered uncontrollably.

In fact, I was so cold that I put on warm clothes, which I never do. Then I closed the window, which I never do, either. I ventured downstairs, fully believing that I was heading for the kitchen to cook something hot for breakfast. I was surprised when I realized which direction my feet had turned—I was out the side door, and heading into Grandma's shop.

As I opened the door, bolts of lightning flashed in the distance, illuminating the place before I could flick on the light. I could see the glass beast reflecting that cold white flash. Then, just before the lightning bolt vanished, I caught a glimpse of my creature's eyes staring at me.

Quickly I turned on the light. My glass beast stood there just as beautiful and menacing as it had the day before, hunched and ready to spring. It leered at me with its large eyes and many rows of teeth. As I neared it, looking deep into its glassy mouth, I swear that I could smell its breath, all salty and wet, like the sea. I moved my hands across it. It was cold as ice and smooth as whalebone. I slid my fingers down the ridges of its curved back, feeling its crystalline sharpness. Then, leaning toward it, I whispered . . . *"I made you."*

Saying it somehow made me feel powerful. "I *created* you," I said, my voice stronger this time. Then, as I peered into its clear glass heart, I thought I saw something move . . . but it was only the reflection of Grandma opening the door behind me.

"Philip, what are you doing here?" she asked. "We don't open for an hour."

I turned to her with a start, feeling a bit embarrassed and guilty for being caught admiring my own handiwork.

"Come have breakfast," she said with a grin. "It'll still be there when you come back."

Then the look on her face changed. It became curious, then concerned. She walked closer to her prize showcase where her most precious creations were kept—colorful swans, dainty unicorns, and other kinds of graceful creatures—and the concern on her face deepened. Something wasn't right in that case, and I realized what it was the same moment that Grandma did.

Every one of her most precious creations was missing its head.

I looked into my grandmother's face and saw a look that wasn't anger—it was sorrow. In fact, it was pain. "Philip, what did you do?" she exclaimed.

My first response was the same sorrow as hers, but it was quickly overcome by fury. I grit my teeth and felt my face going red. "Why do you think it was me?" I shouted, my voice practically a growl.

Her eyes were full of tears. "Who else was in this shop, Philip? All the windows are locked. Do you think neighborhood kids would come in here and do such a thing? No—we have nice children in this neighborhood—*nice* children," she repeated, as if I wasn't one of them. It made me furious. It made me want to take what was left of those pretty glass sculptures and wreck them all.

"Maybe somebody did it before you left yesterday!" I shouted. "Maybe they were like that half the afternoon, and you just didn't notice. How often do you look over there, Grandma?" I stared her down. "How often?"

She looked away, proving that I had won, but I didn't let up.

"Why would I do something like that to you, Grandma?" I pressed, and then I thought back to that first week when I smashed that whole shelf of figurines. "I mean . . . why would I do that *now*? I like it here. I don't want to get sent away."

That clinched it. She finally believed me. One thing about grandparents, when you give them the truth, they can tell. Still, the question remained: Who broke the heads off those figures?

"I guess it must have been some tourist kids," Grandma finally said, shaking her head. Then she headed for the door. "Come have breakfast," she said as she left, not saying another word about it.

I could have believed it, too—that it was some bored tourist kids. I could have believed that there were people mean enough to do things like that . . . because at times I had been one of them. But somewhere deep down, even though I couldn't admit it to myself quite yet, I knew the answer was much closer to home. And as I sat down quietly to eat my bowl of cereal, I couldn't help but think back to my crystalline creation on the heavy wooden counter . . . and how, as I had left the little shop, I could swear it winked at me.

We sold it that afternoon. I was kind of upset. I never thought it would actually sell. If I did, I would have hidden it. It was mine, and I had no desire to see it in someone else's hands. But a large man with a big black hat took one look at it, let out a deep belly laugh, and slapped his fat wallet on the counter. "How much?" he asked.

I swallowed hard. "It's not for sale," I told him. Maybe I didn't say it forcefully enough.

"Name your price," he countered.

Then Grandma had to open her mouth, thinking she was doing me a favor. "Two-hundred-and-fifty dollars," she said. "Not a penny less."

The man raised an eyebrow.

I sighed with relief, certain that no one would pay that much for a piece of glass.

But the man pulled out the cash, placed it in my grandmother's hands, and she placed it in mine. "You earned this," she said proudly.

The man laughed out loud again. "Never seen something so ugly that looked so beautiful," he said. "My wife'll kill me." And then he laughed once more as he carried out my prize beast.

As it turned out, his wife never had the chance to kill him.

Whatever happened, happened sometime during the night. All I know is that the next day the papers said something about a man disappearing. They didn't have a picture yet, but I knew who it was. Even before I read the papers, I knew.

You see, that morning I awoke with a spot of sunlight reflecting in my eyes from a piece of sculptured glass sitting on my dresser. It was my own grinning glass beast.

Again, I had left my window open and was half frozen. My teeth were practically chattering out of my head. I wanted to scream in terror when I saw that my creation was back . . . but at the same time I was glad to see it.

As I stared at the glass beast, I could swear that it was closer to me than it originally was. Was it creating some optical illusion the way it did back when it was just weird sand in the Sand-Trap?

No, I finally decided, it wasn't closer—it was . . . *larger*. At least six inches larger than before. And it wasn't just taller, either. It was broader, as well, and its muscles were thicker than those I had given it. In fact, now I could even see fine glass ridges, like tiny veins, in its huge, bulging muscles.

"Come down for breakfast, Philip!" Grandma called from downstairs.

I looked at the thing, wanting to hate it, wanting to tell it to go away. But I couldn't. The truth was that I didn't want it to go away.

"I can't let her see you," I told my beast, "so I'm going to lock you in here, okay?" Not waiting for an answer—afraid I might actually get one—I quickly left and locked my door.

After school, I went straight to the shop. I didn't want to think about the glass beast in my room. I just wanted to sit there at the register and smile mindlessly for what few tourists and passersby came into the shop on that cold September day.

As I walked in, Grandma gave me a big smile. "You little sneak," she said, wagging her finger at me. "To think you kept it from me all this time!"

I didn't know what she was talking about, and I've learned the best thing to do when you're clueless is to keep your mouth shut until you have a clue.

"I needed to get into your room to collect your dirty laundry, and I was wondering why you locked your door," she went on with a grin. "Anyway, I used my old passkey, and do you know what I found in there?"

I gulped a gallon of air. "What?"

"This," she said and pointed to the showcase that used to hold her now-headless creations. In their place was a large, crystalline punch bowl carved with such care and sharp precision, it looked like it had been cut out of diamond. It must have cost thousands of dollars.

"When'd you buy this?" I asked her, staring at the rim of the bowl, which had fine beveled edges . . . like teeth.

She laughed. "Stop trying to be funny, Philip. I know that you made it. I just didn't realize how talented you were!" she exclaimed, giving me a hug. "Tell me, how long have you been hiding this masterpiece in your room?"

All I could do was keep silent, trying to figure out what was going on.

I looked at the bowl's perfect surface, each cut like a gemstone; its shape perfectly round. I could never make anything like this. Still, there was something familiar about it. I touched it, running my finger down a deep ridge in its surface design.

Cold as ice, I thought. *Smooth as whalebone.*

Then I shuddered so hard I shook nearly every piece of glass in the room.

But Grandma didn't even notice. She was busy putting a five-hundred-dollar price tag on the punch bowl.

It sold that same day to a couple driving south, whose names I made a point to forget.

With my bedroom window open, I waited for it that night. The temperature had dropped, and I could feel myself almost disappearing into the cold.

I heard it before I saw it—a hissing, slithering sound like a snake. Then a long trail of icy liquid glass slithered through the window, down the cold, coiled radiator, across the wall, and onto my dresser.

So perfect, I thought. *So beautiful.* And then I let myself relax, like a father who had been waiting for his child to return home.

Fascinated, I watched it take shape once more—its old shape—the beast I had created. I fell asleep staring at it across the room, mesmerized at how the moon, its blue light twisting through the flapping blinds of my open window, painted my beast in fine neon lines.

In the morning when I awoke, it was something new. A chandelier, with glass arms, and dangling from those arms were a hundred beautifully-shaped, sharp crystalline spears. It was too heavy for me to carry down the stairs all by myself, but somehow I managed it—probably because the chandelier's many arms actually helped itself through the hall, like the arms of an octopus.

Grandma looked at it with a sense of apprehension and a vague sense of dread—the kind of dread you feel before you know enough to feel real fear.

"You . . . you *made* this?" she asked.

"Of course I did, Grandma."

She looked into my eyes, trying to catch me in a lie, but she couldn't, because in a way, I wasn't lying.

"You must have worked all night," she said to me coolly.

"No," I told her. "Actually this is something I've been working on for a while. I've been, uh, hiding it . . . like the punch bowl."

"You've been hiding a lot of things from me in that room," she said.

When I just shrugged, she let it go. I knew she was fishing for a lie, but she found only half-truths. Lucky for Grandma she was a firm believer in old sayings like "What you don't know can't hurt you" and "Let sleeping dogs lie."

I strung the chandelier up from a beam in the corner of the shop, and all day long its dangling crystals sang in the breeze like a wind chime whenever someone walked in. It was as if the thing was trying to draw attention to itself. But it didn't have to do that. Even in the darkest corner of the room it stood out over everything else in the shop.

It was Mr. Dalton who took an interest in it later that day. He owned an antiques shop a few miles down the road, and usually kept his nose too high in the air to step into a tourist shop like ours. But that nose must have gotten wind of some unusual glass sculptures we'd had in the shop lately, because he'd been here twice, earlier in the day, and here he was sniffing around again.

He'd come in first at around ten, pretending not to look at the chandelier, then again after lunch, with a magnifying glass. Finally he returned a third time as we were getting ready to close for the evening, clearly ready to talk business.

"How much do you want for it?" he asked as he ran his finger along its six glass arms, marveling at the fine cut design of its dangling shards, each sharp as a razor.

"It's not for sale, Mr. Dalton," said Grandma without even looking at it. "It's—"

"Seven hundred dollars," I blurted out. It was mine, and I could sell it if I wanted to. Or at least I could "rent" it.

Mr. Dalton laughed a practiced laugh—the kind he gave whenever he was bargaining with someone.

"Come, now," he said. "Don't be ridiculous, son. After all, it may be unique, but it's full of imperfections. There are flaws in the design, and—"

"No, there aren't," I countered, staring him straight in the eye. "It's perfect . . . absolutely perfect. Seven hundred dollars, or no deal."

He grit his teeth through his congenial smile, furious to be out-bargained by a thirteen-year-old. "Very well," he said. Then he paid me in cash, probably figuring he would sell it in his own shop for over a thousand.

As I helped Mr. Dalton carry the chandelier out of the shop, Grandma looked at me, trying to read something in my face. But lately it seemed my face was unreadable, even to me as I stared at myself in the mirror each morning.

"Would you mind riding with me to my store?" Mr. Dalton asked after we'd put the chandelier into the back of his van. "I could sure use your help carrying it in."

Figuring he'd sort of paid for my help already, I hopped into the front seat, and we took off.

It was as I was carrying the chandelier from Mr. Dalton's van to his shop that I thought I heard it breathe through the tinkling of its many dangling crystals. It sounded like the rush of the ocean when you put your ear to a shell.

Once inside Dalton's shop, we hoisted the chandelier up with a rope over a beam, right in the center of the room. It took a while, and by the time we were done, it was already dark outside. The antiques shop was lit with dim yellow incandescent lights that glimmered off the hanging chandelier, casting tiny spots of light around the room like fireflies.

I hung around, waiting for something to happen.

"It's not that far," Mr. Dalton said to me after a few moments. "I suspect you can walk home from here."

I shrugged, glanced at the chandelier again, and waited.

"I hope you don't think you're getting a tip for bringing it over," he said coldly. "I've already paid through the nose as it is."

And that's when it happened. The crystalline monstrosity jerked itself off the rope and fell.

Spinning out of the way just in time, Mr. Dalton looked with wonder, which quickly built into horror, at the chandelier. It had landed on the ground like a cat, barely making a sound. Then, two crystalline spheres hanging in its center turned toward the terrified man. And both he and I knew at that moment that those spheres were the thing's eyes.

Amazed, I watched it skitter on the wooden floor like a giant glass spider, then spring across the room, landing right on top of Mr. Dalton. He sputtered something I couldn't hear, but he didn't have a chance to scream as the chandelier's glass arms swung inward, and its hundred dangling crystals became teeth as sharp as the shards of a broken bottle.

It was feeding.

I couldn't watch a moment longer, and I ran to the next room, stumbling over furniture, smashing my shins. Quickly I slammed the door behind me, then collapsing in an old high-backed chair, I turned the chair around so I didn't even have to see the door.

That's when I spotted an old-time radio, large and wooden, across the room. I raced over and turned it on, found a station, and cranked up the music full blast, drowning out the sounds coming from the other room. For five minutes I sat there . . . then ten . . . then twenty. Finally I dared to turn off the radio.

There was silence in the other room, and soon my curiosity began to match my fear. Slowly I made my way back in, opening the creaking door, terrified of what I might see.

But when I finally looked in, I saw no sign of Mr. Dalton—not a button, not a shoelace . . . and the creature— my creature—sat there in the very center of the room. It had resumed its old form now—the gargoyle beast that I had first created. I could hear it breathing a heavy satisfied breath, and I could see its chest rising and falling.

Slowly the beast moved toward me, but I didn't run. My feet were frozen, and I couldn't move. It came up close and brushed against me, purring like a cat. I reached out and stroked its icy mane. The second I touched it, my fear began to drain away, replaced by numbness. In fact, I could feel the creature draining away everything I had ever felt. Everything good, everything bad—all of it was slipping away into a cold emptiness. It was like sinking into quicksand.

Am I its master? I wondered. *Or is it the other way around?*

As the monster circled around me, I could see just how big it had grown. It was as big as me now, and I felt helplessly drawn to it.

I climbed on its back, and it leapt out an open window,

carrying me home with such powerful smooth strides, it felt like I was floating on air. I could almost feel myself dissolving into it, becoming a part of it.

Grandma never mentioned the crystalline beast to me or to anyone. She didn't even say a word about it when the police came by to see if we had seen Mr. Dalton on the day he had disappeared. We told the officers the truth—that the man had bought a chandelier, and that I had helped him carry it back to his place.

That was a month ago, although it feels like another lifetime. In fact, everything that came before my creature feels like another lifetime to me now.

Grandma doesn't talk to me much anymore. She tolerates me in the house, and at the breakfast table. She'll ask me to pass the butter and stuff, but she takes no further interest in my comings and goings . . . or to the comings and goings of other things in the house. She asks no questions, and locks herself in her room most of the time. Perhaps I should feel bad about that, but I don't feel much of anything anymore. Except cold.

My dad came to visit today, with his girlfriend, who I've been told is now my stepmom. She's the same one who first suggested I be sent away to live here—the same one who convinced him that a college fund for me was unrealistic, and the money was better spent on their summer trip to Europe.

Dad's out jogging now, and my new stepmom is upstairs drawing a bath. "Oh, how beautiful," she'd said when she'd first stepped into the guest bathroom. "A bathtub made entirely of glass!"

"They don't make them like this anymore," I had told her, running my fingers along the art-deco design of its sharp beveled edges.

Now I sit downstairs listening to loud music. I am icy cold as I let the music flow through me, like the icy wind blowing through the window that I always keep open. My veins are like glass, growing numb, and I feel myself feeling nothing . . . while upstairs, my beautiful crystalline bathtub slowly fills with water.